Bloom

The Next Generation

Deborah D'Antonio

Dedication

When we heal ourselves from wounds,
we heal our ancestors.
When our ancestors are healed,
we heal the wounds of humanity.

Table of Contents

"Your children are not your children,
They are sons and daughters of life's longing
for itself.

They come through you but not from you.
And though they are with you, yet they belong
not to you.

You may give them your love but not your thoughts,
for they have their own thoughts.

You may house their bodies but not their souls,
For their souls dwell in the house of tomorrow,
which you cannot visit, not even in your dreams.

You may strive to be like them
but seek not to make them like you.

For life goes not backward nor tarries with
yesterday.

You are the bows from which your children as
living arrows are sent forth..."
- Khalil Gibran

Introduction

*G*od designed his world for generations of family. Ephesians teaches that man was not created because the woman needed him; the woman was created because the man needed her. Neither is woman inferior to man nor is man inferior to woman. For just as woman was taken from the side of the man, in the same way man is taken from the womb of the woman.

The *Psalms* teach that He commanded our fathers to teach their children so that a future generation of children, yet to be born, might know that they were to rise to tell their children.

It's a passing of the baton to the next generation or the analogy of handing them a master key or a password that is a secret to be shared with family only. Then, the older generation joins their ancestors, and the cycle continues in the values of their traditions.

If you look deeply in the palm of your hand, you will see your parents and your ancestors. Each is present in your body as you are a continuation of each one. Our grandparents planted seeds in us when they knew they would never live to see the end result of the legacy they shared, learning wisdom that only time taught them.

This is a story of our next generation, and we will start with our parents, Steve and Kate, that are in heaven. The book you are holding in your hand is a sequel to the first of the series titled *First Kiss, Last Kiss.*

We were blessed and strive to instill the same values to our children taught by their ancestors before them. Their roots since time began take seed and root.

We are three brothers Luca, Jesse, and David. *First Kiss, Last Kiss* tells you about us as boys and men and our families in the early years. Our mother, Kate, taught us that it is through our families that we learn love, and in learning love, we find God.

We are sharing the story of our children becoming: THE NEXT GENER-ATION.

Chapter One

David and Darla - The Denari Family

Danielle and Daphne were the oldest of David and Darla's children. Next came Dakota and Drew that were bossed around by their two older sisters. The boys were happy when Dena was born because they could in turn have someone to boss around.

All in all, they were a good bunch of kids. They all had dark hair and big dark eyes like their parents. People used to remark that they all looked alike and should be models. They also had a family dog and of course named him Duke. After all it started with the letter D, right?

When the boys grew older, towering over their sisters in height, their older sisters, Danielle and Daphne, stopped telling them what to do, which was a pretty smart move on their part. So, they all started to baby the youngest, Dena.

When the boys started coming around, Dakota and Drew were very protective of their sisters which made their father David's job a lot easier. They both spent time at the gym and were powerfully built. They could appear intimidating.

Dakota and Drew were very athletic and played varsity football and baseball in high school and college. They were both team players and the coaches through the years appreciated their dedication. Danielle and Daphne were on the dance team and had years of training in gymnastics. Danielle was very intelligent and outgoing with a great sense of humor. Daphne was the total opposite. David said Daphne was his fragile flower. She was very intuitive and felt things around her deeply.

The youngest, Dena, started ballet classes at three and her dream was to become a prima ballerina. She was an exceptional dancer and was even chosen to study with a principal dancer from the Bolshoi ballet. Her name was Natasha Ristov, visiting from Russia, and Dena was in awe of her. Natasha watched Dena perform as the soloist in Swan Lake and afterwards invited her to a summer intensive in Russia where Miss Ristov would make sure she had the proper training.

She also told Dena she would need to get used to very sore toes. Dena was so excited that she felt like she was walking on air and couldn't even feel her toes!

Dakota and Drew were both at university now. Dakota was pre-med and hoped to become a pediatric surgeon like his Uncle Luca.

Drew's dream was to become an architect. He had a very creative mind and loved to sketch new ideas. He was truly a visionary. Danielle started her first year at university and was on the swim team. She was undecided about her future. She was having fun making new friends and kidded her parents that she studied in her free time. However, her sophomore year she decided to be a lawyer like her father, which made David ecstatic. He knew she would be a fine lawyer and Darla agreed.

Daphne was finishing her last year of high school and all her hours of music lessons were starting to show, but she seemed to have exceptional talent playing the violin. She even started writing music. Her music teacher encouraged her to keep at it in college as she felt it would lead to an amazing career.

All the siblings loved their cousins and looked forward to all the family vacations that were always a riot. They stayed close in touch and even more so since they got older. They envied Uncle Luca and Diane's family living in the south, especially with their cold Midwestern winters.

Living on the beach everyday had to be amazing. Their cousins taught them to surf and had beach parties with their friends when they visited. However, their southern cousins said the Midwest had its charm and visited often to ski, snowboard and ice skate. They were all very athletic.

Uncle Jesse and Tante Gabrielle lived in Seattle with their cousin Jax, which was an amazing place.

Jax said you had to get used to it raining almost daily in some seasons, which they called misting.

So, the cousins had the best of all worlds visiting back and forth. They loved when all the aunties and uncles called them "the next generation." They were all so proud of their family.

David and Darla were winding down one night relaxing together with some wine on a cold winter evening by the fire. David thought how blessed he was to have Darla as his wife. She still looked beautiful with her bright eyes that always seemed to sparkle and was an outstanding mother.

Darla was still crazy in love with her handsome husband and they both adored their family with the exception of their boxer, Duke. He was getting old, cranky, and barking at everything which drove them bonkers. But truthfully, the whole family would be lost without him.

They marveled through the years watching each of their children struggle or excel at different things in life. They both felt strongly about letting them pick the direction they would choose in life and thanked God for their blessings.

The kids gave them some moments with lots of grounding, but they all had good grades, good friends, and loved each other. What more could parents ask for in life?

David was drifting asleep warmed by the fire and thinking of his parents, Kate and Steve, more than usual, and how proud they would be at how close all the family stuck together. They taught them that nothing was more important than family and David agreed. Each generation to leave that important message to the next.

When David woke up, he had a call from Jax to fly down immediately. Jesse was in the hospital.

Chapter Two

The Gianni Family

It was a brilliant balmy wonderful Saturday at the beach and the Gianni family was very loud as usual.

The boys were all home and Diane was making their favorites for lunch to celebrate being together.

Kathleen offered to help but Diane told her to go get some sunshine and she would have one of her brothers come get her when it was ready. Diane understood how hard the last year of college is with finals. Kathleen wanted to go on to get a Master's in Social Work. She was extremely bright as was her mother, Shannon.

Kathleen had been the most outstanding daughter and Diane would always be grateful to her mother Shannon for signing adoption papers to make Kathleen her daughter before she died. She missed her dear friend and knew Kathleen always had a sadness about her since it happened. Kathleen always had a dream to visit Ireland one day and Diane promised to make that happen.

Kathleen started calling Diane and Luca Momma and Dad like the boys years ago. She looked so much like Diane that it was uncanny. Shannon used to tell Diane that Kathleen's dad could have passed for her brother. Kathleen was deeply in love with Jesse and Gabrielle's son, Jax, and truth be told, Diane and Luca were relieved they weren't blood relatives. They loved Jax too.

Diane gave all the boys names that pertained to the sea. The boys thought that was hilarious! When they got older the girls thought it was *very cool.* None of the boys had serious relationships yet. They brought home some interesting girls and Luca and Diane shared some laughs how their sons tried to act *dignified* around them.

Dylan would be finishing up at university the following year. He actually to their surprise, being the most ornery in the family, wanted to attend seminary to become a chaplain. Dylan was an English name meaning *son of the sea waves,* and that boy was riding the waves surfing since he could barely walk.

Diane actually thought he was joking, but when she thought about it, he was always the one to befriend someone that was being picked on at school or comfort Kathleen when she was missing her birth mother. A thousand other memories started resurfacing too. Diane could see Luca's personality in her son, but he was the exact image of his Uncle Jesse.

Kai, the second born, joined the navy and his siblings teased him because his name was a Hawaiian name for sea. Kai favored Luca in looks with the same muscular build. He could be a handful but a sweetheart underneath his bravado.

Diane wasn't happy about his choice to join the military but grateful it wasn't war time. She remembered what Jesse and so many others went through in Vietnam. Kathleen tried to talk him out of it because her father, Liam, was killed in Vietnam when she was very young.

Alon had a Filipino name that simply meant *waves*. Her third born was starting veterinarian school, which was no surprise, as he brought every stray animal home for as long as she could remember. If Alon had his way their house would look more like a petting zoo. Alon favored both Luca and Diane in looks but with a very slender build.

The baby of the family, that they all totally spoiled rotten, was named Brodny, a Slavic name which meant *a person dwelling near a stream*. The name was perfect for him because he had a fishing pole in his hand since birth, which Luca loved. When Diane's father visited, they would always take off to the pier. He actually looked like Diane's father Pastor Mike, slim with light hair and dark eyes.

Diane's parents visited often and adored the grandkids. They were getting up in age and there was a cottage for sale a block away. For their sixtieth wedding anniversary Luca and Diane bought them the cottage. It would be better for them to live in a warmer climate, and they would be happy for the kids to spend time with the older generation. Diane and Luca wished their other grandparents, Steve and Kate, were still alive. The cycle of life, each generation sharing with the next.

The house was very quiet when all the kids left the next morning. Diane kissed Luca, handed him a cup of coffee, and said she was going outside for a walk. The sunrise was stunning. She never got tired of living on the beach and hearing the sound of laughter and children making sandcastles. Diane knew how blessed she was, and Luca was the best father and husband.

She didn't know if it was adjusting to the kids being away, but her heart felt heavy. She started having strange dreams about Jesse reaching out for her the last few weeks. Luca said she was crying in her sleep and then one morning it happened. She received a phone call from Gabrielle, telling her that Jesse was dying in the hospital.

Luca had already left for work and had two surgeries that day, so she booked a flight to go see Jesse. She contacted Luca and the plan was that Luca would come the following day, but it was going to be too late.

Chapter Three

Jesse, Gabrielle, and Jax Denari

Narrated by Jax

Growing up in my family was great. If I could have changed one thing though, it would have been to have a brother or sister. But it turned out my cousins are like brothers and sisters to me, and we have always had the best times together.

My parents are both doctors. My mom, Gabrielle's family was killed in church one day in Vietnam. She wasn't feeling well so she didn't go that morning. She had a very tragic upbringing but is a very strong woman and dedicated mother.

My dad is the most caring father a guy could ever ask for, and we have had so many amazing father and son times together. His patients all love him and tell me how lucky I am to be his son. I think so too.

He taught me many things that he learned as a combat soldier. He said my mother saved him in the war by healing him. He also said she gave him the best gift in life which was me. So, we were a small family but a happy one including our goofy lovable big dog, Rocco. He is a huge Golden Retriever and thinks he is a puppy.

I was also one lucky boy with grandparents. My dad's parents, Steve and

Kate, spoiled me, and I loved every second. I never met two kinder people. My Grandfather Steve said Grandma Kate made him fat. He never seemed to turn down anything she prepared, which made me laugh. So, life was good until it wasn't. If I was to guess when it happened, it was when my dad went to his hometown to a friend's wedding. I had scout camp that weekend and Mom told him to go have fun and stop to see his parents. My father was excited to see all his friends from high school.

When Dad came back, he was very quiet. Mom asked him what was wrong, but he told her he was fine. Then he started looking pale and constantly going for blood tests that showed nothing. He wasn't even excited cheering me on at my games. This was definitely not like my dad!

I heard my mom talking to a friend on the phone that she was going to demand that he tell her what the problem was. She was tired of him moping around the house.

That night I heard them get in a big fight and I ran to my room because it scared me. After that, nothing was ever the same.

I called my Grandma Kate, but she didn't know what was wrong either. Later that night, Dad called Grandma and I kept hearing him tell her about someone named Diane.

When I asked my mom who Diane was, she looked very angry, but said she had no idea. I never believed her but was taught to respect my parents.

We went on a family vacation to the Blue Ridge Mountains. I was so excited to see my Uncle David and Aunt Darla's kids and got to meet my Uncle Luca's kids too.

Grandma recently found out Luca was her adopted son. His wife's name was Diane and I wondered if somehow this could be the same Diane, as she and Grandma seemed very close. Dad and Diane looked at one another like they had a secret and it made me feel funny inside.

The next morning, I met my oldest cousin, Kathleen. We weren't blood related as Luca and Diane adopted her when her mother died from cancer.

When I saw her, I kept smiling at her and kept trying to stop acting like an idiot, but it was no use. She was very beautiful, and it was hard not to stare. We got to know each other, and it was all over for me. As luck would have it, she felt the same way. I would never have this feeling with another girl. Even though I was young, I just knew it.

Kathleen and I became very close, and years later we still feel the same way. I was going to propose when we finished college. I am presently finishing school for my MBA degree.

Then life struck our family hard. My grandparents, Steve and Kate, died within a short time of each other. It was a sad reunion this time for the Denari-Gianni families. The only time my dad seemed content is when our families were together, and he and Diane still looked like they shared a secret. This didn't seem to go unnoticed by my mother.

My mother seemed angry all the time and Dad seemed depressed. One day my dad started to get high fevers and started coughing up blood. He was taken by ambulance and admitted to the hospital. My Uncle David and I rarely left his side. He was going downhill fast and for the first time I thought my dad might be dying. I felt afraid.

His last conversation to me was to never give up if you love someone. Then he told me the story about Mom getting pregnant with me, and that he loved Diane since they were teens. I am not sure if he would have told me that if his fever wasn't so high. He was really out of it.

My Uncle David was in the room when my father told me about Diane. He seemed to have known about it the whole time. I felt like I ruined my dad's life.

My Aunt Diane was in the hall outside Dad's room when I walked out. I told her that I was so sorry to ruin her life with my dad. My Aunt sat me down and told me I was the best thing that ever happened to my father and gave me the biggest hug. She said her life was with her children and my Uncle Luca. Then she told me to call Kathleen. My auntie knew that Kathleen had a calming effect on me.

I planned to call Kathleen anyway and then go back to see my dad. I didn't want to stay away from him for very long, but I needed to get myself together.

Chapter Four

Jesse's Journey Home

Jesse Narrates

So, this was it I thought. Diane was still holding my hand when David and Jax walked in behind my friend, Dr. Ross, who was on call. He examined me, then pronounced me dead, and looked very sad. I could see and hear everything in the room.

He was a good friend for many years and one of the first doctors to join our practice at the clinic. With tears in his eyes, he patted my shoulder and extended his sympathy to my family. He told them to take their time, closed the door, and left them to some privacy.

All three appeared to be in shock. Jax was crying for the longest time with his head on my chest and then tried to reach his mother, but she didn't answer. My brother David started sobbing and told me to fly free, then totally broke down. Diane was stoic and never moved, as though she was transfixed to the spot. I think she could feel my spirit in the room and the love that remained.

I started to feel a pull and took one last look at the three people I loved the most still on earth, my love Diane, my boy Jax, and baby brother David.

I started to become very aware of two angels on either side of me. I heard two loud pops and felt as though I was being lifted up through my head somehow. I was floating in the sky and had an odd thought that it was a beautiful day to die. The birds were sweetly singing in a bright, cornflower blue sky with white fluffy clouds floating by, as I said goodbye to my earthly home. I wondered if God's little creatures in the air could see us.

I was protected by two angels that appeared to be about nine feet tall. It was at that moment they allowed me to see them. I recognized them from many years ago during a psychotherapy session. They seemed to be twins that had more of a male presence, and comedic in nature. I wondered at the time if they were actually taking their jobs as guardians seriously. I understood now that they protected me all my life, especially in Vietnam.

One was a witnessing angel and the other a recording angel; it was their job to take me safely on my journey home to heaven. They were beings of colorful rays of intense light. Every time they moved, I saw colors of shimmering lights with harmonic musical sounds emanating around them. They were more like dancing light than form. They communicated through thought to my spirit and never spoke in words.

I remembered a verse from many years ago in Exodus 23:20. *Behold I send an angel before you to keep you in the way and bring you into the place I have prepared.* The angels exuded compassion, care, and safety.

Just then we broke through the earth's atmosphere in an explosion enveloped in deep velvet indigo darkness. I was floating in quiet stillness and awestruck wonder, never feeling fear, but to the contrary--total love. It could be described as swimming in gentle waves of emptiness and silence.

I could see enormous galaxies with brilliant colors I had never seen! I felt enveloped in majestic lights that were so enormously expansive. It was like being wrapped in a soft blanket filled with love and peace in the midst of the cosmos. We seemed to be moving at a tremendous speed now with a bright light up ahead.

The freeing joy I felt was something never experienced at this level on earth. It was a mysterious awareness of infinity. I think it would be torture to have this feeling and return to a sick body again.

More joy mixed with profound love filled my spirit, and what I saw next was ecstasy. The white light was love itself, and intelligence that permeated everything as a light within. When I looked at my hand, light went straight through it.

Everyone and everything was bathed in light.

I saw magnificent garden meadows filled with radiant flowers. Some I recognized but most I didn't. Little children were laughing and playing games, knee deep in emerald green grass.

There were beautiful trees swaying in the breeze. Everything was alive with a degree of love I had never felt on earth. Even the fragrant scents were other worldly where all of nature breathed!

A river seemed to run through the middle of the city, like a sheet of pale blue sea glass. The streets were paved with smooth crystals made from amethyst, emeralds, sapphires, and jasper. It was truly a *Crystal City* where golden light sparkled like twinkling, shimmering diamonds.

The angels did their job getting me through the gate and pointed up ahead. I communicated my deep profound love and gratitude to them. Once again, their humorous personalities came through and I had to smile.

They reminded me of some hilarious times in my life. Apparently, I had fun angels and wondered if Diane did also, the way we use to laugh. They nodded their agreement knowing my thoughts. They communicated that we knew each other before our time on earth and both totally understood the deep meaning of sacred love.

There was a large hall filled with people on massage tables, while angels administered magnetic treatments that appeared somewhat like what Gabrielle did. I was told these people were being revived from years of torturous lives they endured, and their spirits were exhausted.

There was another building where the greatest healers of all times gathered together next to a glass building. It appeared to be a higher learning center library with many steps to the entrance. Up ahead was a Hall of Music that had beautiful melodic vibrations coming through the stained-glass windows. The sounds filled my whole being with blissful delight.

Joy bubbled up in me at what I saw next. There was a huge gathering of family and friends welcoming me. My mother and father hugged me, followed by Poppy, my granddad that died when I was ten. My Uncle Nicky and Aunt Helen were next. Everyone looked so young, maybe in their thirties.

When I didn't think I could hold anymore love, my little dog, Baxter, from childhood came wagging his tail. My buddies from Vietnam were looking out for him for me. How I missed my best buddy Ben, Pete, the man of great faith, and Achak, my Navajo Indian friend. There were so many people rejoicing my arrival, and to my surprise I seemed to recognize many of their faces, but not entirely sure how. There were billions of peace-filled lights shining from other souls everywhere.

Then I was led by my precious mother to a winding stairway, with tenderness in her eyes and a sweet smile on her face, encouraging me to go ahead.

When I reached the top, I felt a love deep in my soul that let me know I belonged, enveloped in love, breathing in grace, and eternal ecstasy.

That's when I saw Him. The Presence of Love in all totality. My Creator. The One that made me! His true divine essence. It was euphoric and I got down on my knees before Him.

God is brilliance bathed in light. His one light connected to all of life. God is Love in its highest purest form. It was this very moment my soul felt complete. I am Home!

Chapter Five

David Walks to a Nearby Park

$\mathcal{I}$ had to call Darla so she could let our family know the news but first I had to calm down and clear my mind. I walked to the park that was near the hospital. I couldn't help thinking how my brother could die on such a beautiful day. Such a random silly thought. After walking a little I realized how exhausted I was and sat on a bench. I noticed my shoulders being stiff and a headache coming on.

For as far back as I could remember, Jesse was my idol, the big brother that always looked out for me. I felt numb even though I knew this was coming. I also felt angry that my brother tried to be a fair and good person his whole life and ended up basically dying from a broken heart. He confided something to me years ago but swore me to secrecy, especially from Diane.

At Bradley and Cyrena's wedding he spent time with Diane and knew he loved her more than ever. If anything, their bond was even stronger. They both felt broken-hearted. Diane wasn't married at the time, but she was too decent to cheat with a married man. Jesse knew it wasn't right either. He wanted to be a better example to his son Jax.

When Jesse got home from the wedding, he felt so defeated and guilty that he wasn't able to love Gabrielle the way a man should love his wife.

He seemed to lose interest in the things that gave him joy, even watching Jax play sports. He started turning down invitations to their friends' gatherings which was so out of character for him.

Gabrielle kept asking him what was wrong and finally one evening he confessed the problem to her and asked for a divorce. He was shocked by her reaction. She simply said that she would never give him a divorce and if he tried to go through with it, she would make sure Jax hated him.

My brother was totally speechless as this was so out of character for Gabrielle. He told me maybe when Jax started college he would leave but knew it would be selfish asking Diane to wait. He had put her through enough heartbreak already.

When we found out that Luca was our adopted brother, Jesse's health went downhill. What were the chances that his own brother, with all the other women in the world, would find Diane to marry? He grew to love Luca, and knew it had to be over with Diane forever.

I used to watch him at family reunions, and he was so grateful just to be near Diane. I know it was mutual but neither of them would ever hurt Luca.

And now he was gone. I am sure my mom and dad are welcoming my brother home with open arms.

He will always be my hero.

Chapter Six

Arriving at Jesse's Funeral

The Denari-Gianni family were all grief stricken.

The males were all dressed in black suits and ties, with gleaming white shirts. The women all looked elegant in black suits and Gabrielle wore a black hat with a sheer black veil partly covering her face.

The girls were all dressed in white suits and dresses. It made a striking contrast to the men.

They looked stunning and drew strength from one another. Much credit was due to Steve and Kate, the generation before, leaving an imprint on their three sons and their families.

Most of the grandchildren were old enough to remember them with joyous, love-filled memories, and everyone in the family knew they were with them in spirit today.

It was a warm spring day filled with sunshine and bright turquoise blue skies. Jesse's grave would be on the north side of the cemetery. It was on a hill that overlooked a lush forest where you could see people jogging, and riding bikes. You could hear the laughter of children so full of life, in contrast to the stillness of the cemetery.

Everything seemed to be in place to honor Jesse. There were rows and rows of white chairs lined up in the hundreds. He would have been so touched to see so many of his army buddies. They shared an unbroken bond of brotherhood, like family in every sense of the word.

The soft, green grass was dewy, sparkling in the gentle breeze. There was a huge crowd of people walking in to pay their respects. Military, patients from the clinic, friends, and neighbors came to say goodbye to their friend. His family's loss was immense.

Gabrielle had already called the chaplain to inform him of a few men that would be speaking. She rode with David and Darla together in a town car. She insisted Jax go with his cousins as she knew they were a great source of comfort to him. She was feeling many emotions today but proud of herself wasn't one of them.

Chapter Seven

Cuz Crew

Cousins are connected heart to heart,
distance and time can't break them apart.

The cousins were usually a rowdy bunch when they were together, but not today. They all went to the cemetery together in a limo. All the siblings in the car loved their cousins and looked forward to the family vacations that were always a blast. They stayed in close touch and shared everything that was going on in their lives.

The cousins thought living on the beach every day had to be amazing except during hurricane season, of course. For Uncle Luca and Aunt Diane, living in the south, especially during the midwestern winters, had to be incredible.

They even managed to get a few romances started when they got older but the only one that stuck was Jax and Kathleen. Grandma Kate said they reminded her of Jesse and Diane at that age.

The southern cousins said "y'all", and the cousins teased them unmercifully about what "y'all" meant. Then everyone would start in on the correct word "pop" or "soda" depending on what part of the country you lived in.

They all loved to be sarcastic and tease each other, but always in good fun, except Kathleen, but they were working on her. She was, however, coming out of her shell more and more.

She was a more refined, serious person, probably because both her parents died when she was young and then adopted by Uncle Luca and Aunt Diane. She was crazy in love with Jax, and it was mutual.

On their trips to Seattle, Tante Gabrielle took the girls to visit the *Seattle Aquarium* and the lovely *Seattle Art Museum*. The boys voted to stay home playing football with the uncles.

They liked to go together to the famous *Space Needle* and the parks that were filled with beautiful Pacific Rhododendrons, their state flower. They always made time for *Pike Place Market* with their quaint cobblestone streets. They loved to watch the *fish throwers* entertain the crowd by throwing fish weighing up to 15kg. There was amazing food everywhere and musicians on every street corner.

Uncle Jesse enjoyed taking just the kids hiking and paragliding on *Poo Poo Point*, on the shoulder of *West Tiger Mountain*. He could be so silly and lighthearted, making us have giggle fits all day.

The youngest cousins kept saying *Poo Poo Point* with belly laughs. It was hard to believe that our uncle was a combat soldier in Vietnam. He said we are all officially Seattleites now!

When we were lucky, we would get a good view of the *Aurora Borealis* at *Snoqualmie Point* off exit 27 on I90.

So, the cousins had the best of all worlds visiting back and forth. They loved when all the aunties and uncles called them *The Next Generation*. How incredibly sad that of the generation before them, one didn't survive.

Jesse was still young, and they all felt such sadness sitting in near silence riding to the cemetery. The cousins were going to give all their strength and courage to Jax today and Kathleen never let go of his hand.

Chapter Eight

Family Arriving

*Those we love and lose are always connected
by heart strings into infinity.*
-Terri Guillemets

*L*uca and Diane would arrive shortly, as they drove to pick up Diane's parents, Pastor Mike and Emily, and Diane's sister, Molly. Pastor Mike was asked to perform the eulogy. He thought about how close he came to having Jesse as his son-in-law, and how fate sent his daughter to Jesse's brother, Luca.

Molly went directly to David, and they hugged each other tight. They were both feeling very sentimental. David told her that he heard the great news that she was promoted to law professor. "Aww Davey, it was from all those law vibrations being around you as kids."

"Seriously, I am so heartbroken for all of you. Jesse was so good to me, as I shamelessly flirted with him in my nine-year-old girl style, making my sister laugh." They both chuckled and hugged again and Molly went to sit by her mom.

When Luca and Diane went to offer their sympathy, Diane took a deep breath as she didn't know how Gabrielle would react. It had to be embarrassing for her with Jesse crying out to her instead of his wife when he was dying. Gabrielle was gracious but had a very odd expression on her face. When Gabrielle looked into Diane's eyes, she knew with certainty that Jesse didn't confess to Diane about asking for a divorce when he returned from Cyrena and Bradley's wedding. Gabrielle also knew how hard this day was for Diane. She and Jesse were like two parts of a whole.

The hearse arrived and it was arranged that Jesse's nephews would be pall bearers. They all looked like grown men, so handsome and strong. Diane's boys, Dylan, Kai, Alon, and Brodny, along with Darla's sons, Drew and Dakota, all looked somber.

They carried their Uncle Jesse's casket with great care and took their seats next to their sisters Danielle, Daphne, Dena, and Kathleen. Jax sat between Kathleen and his mom. Jax felt as though his mom was very distant. He felt so sad for her.

Kathleen was his rock, and he affirmed once again that someday he would make her his wife. He was always grateful that they weren't blood related.

The chaplain asked everyone to please be seated and the ceremony began. A bagpipe player performed *Amazing Grace* which was very heartfelt. Kathleen and the younger nieces were all crying at this point as were others. It all felt so surreal.

Pastor Mike began the eulogy. "Today I will try to give words to sorrow. We are here to share grief as well as joy in celebrating Jesse Denari. I have known Jesse since he was a teenager and so honored to know him and his incredible family all these years.

"Everyone here will grieve in their own way as we have lost someone precious that will never be replaced. To touch the soul of another human being is to walk on Holy ground.

"Khalil Gibran said, 'And what is to cease breathing but to be free from its restless tide, that it may rise and expand and seek God unencumbered.'

"When Jesse was in Vietnam, he wrote me many times for advice about God. It's a testimony to this man to see the great crowd that came today from many miles away to say goodbye. I know without a doubt that he is in heaven today. Au revoir Jesse. Until we meet again, rest in peace."

The chaplain shook Pastor Mike's hand and announced to the gathering that they had two guest speakers today.

A man with a little girl went to the front. The little girl was precious with golden curls and big brown eyes. She was waving a little American flag in her hand. The man looked very somber and said, "Good morning. My name is Erik, and I was a medic when Jesse and I were in Vietnam. He nicknamed me *the surfer boy from California.*

"We kept in close touch all these years and when my granddaughter was gravely ill, Jesse flew out to help her with a more natural approach, as the medicines the doctors prescribed were too harsh for her little body. He left a busy practice and kept trying different formulas until one started showing improvement. This is my granddaughter, Susan, and she is part of our family's happy ending. Thank you." Erik shook hands with Gabrielle and Jax offering his deepest sympathy, holding the little girl's hand and sat down.

The second speaker was introduced as Sergeant Smitty, Jesse's drill sergeant from AIT. He began, "I heard from one of the men that Jesse kept a journal with the purpose of turning it into a book one day. Jesse even gave it a title, *Vietnam – A Soldier's Story*. His intent was to expose the real truth of what was going on in Vietnam.

"The day he left Vietnam he gave it to a close buddy to finish writing it. To make a long story short the buddy he left it with was my stepbrother. He forgot about it and found it in his attic last year. He has been working on getting it published as a surprise to Jesse.

"We were heartsick to learn he died before we could tell him. The literary agent expects it to be a best seller and the proceeds of the book will go to vets in need." Sergeant Smitty handed the book to Gabrielle. The cover had a sketch of a handsome soldier in uniform carrying his M16 that looked exactly like Jesse. The background had a picturesque scene of Vietnam with helicopters on the top right corner. The illustrator was a vet and wouldn't accept any money for the drawing.

Sergeant Smitty shook Jax's hand and said, "Son, I hope you don't believe everything your father said about me." Jax replied, "Not most of it sir." Both men smiled and Jax added that his father was always grateful to his drill sergeant to prepare him for war. Both men shook hands again and Smitty had tears in his eyes that Jesse still died too young.

✳✳✳✳✳

Completion of Service

The honor guards stood at attention and began to fold the flag. Jax remembered that his father taught him that *Old Glory* had thirteen folds, each having a special meaning.

Next came the three volley shots with rifles. The significance is duty, honor, and sacrifice.

Immediately following, an honor guard played taps on the bugle. Once again Jax had a memory of his dad telling him that there were many versions of how taps originated. He said it dated back to the Civil War.

Union Army Brigadier General Daniel Butterfield wrote the tune and worked with his bugler, Oliver W. Norton, to perfect it. It was then started after the firing of the volleys at funerals. Jax now understood why this melody leaves a lump in your throat and remembered every word.

Day is Done,
Gone the sun,
From the lakes,
From the hills,
From the sky.

All is well,
Safely rest,
God is nigh.
Fading light,
Dims the sight,
And a star,
Gems the sky,
Gleaming bright.
From afar,
Drawing nigh,
Falls the night.

Thanks and praise,

For our days.

Neath the sun,

Neath the stars,

Neath the sky.

As we go,

This we know,

God is nigh.

The guard presented the flag on one knee looking closely at Gabrielle and said: "On behalf of the President of the United States, the United States Army and a grateful nation, please accept this flag as a symbol of our appreciation for your loved one's honorable and faithful service." He then saluted very slowly and walked away.

The chaplain then asked everyone to stand and recite the 23rd Psalm and then began his sermon about family.

"Job 8:10, *But those who came before us will teach you. They will teach you from the wisdom of former generations.* To the Denari-Gianni family, remember Jesse and your ancestors' legacy. Keep the love in your families strong like you were taught. Family is the link to our past and bridge to our future. Other things may change but we start and end with family.

"Your families' future generations will move forward like all before them. May you find strength and support in your love for one another and may peace fill your hearts. Let us leave in quietness of spirit and live with care, love, and concern for one another. The service has ended."

Luca was talking to David, so Diane started to walk ahead. She felt an urge to walk to the end of the hill. She looked from the hill to the forest and to her right she saw a man approaching her.

"Pardon madame." She noticed he was holding a vibrant pink rose. The man continued on with a very thick French accent, "I was bringing flowers to my mother's grave and a man with bright blue eyes handed me this rose. He pointed you out and asked me to give you this message. 'Je t'aime sans limite.' When I turned for one moment he seemed to have vanished into thin air."

Diane felt, then saw Jesse's spirit bathed in bright light behind the man with a big smile and then he was gone.

Leave it to Jesse. The words spoken in French meant that his love had no limits or boundaries.

The flower was exactly like the ones in his mother Kate's garden he would often pick for Diane.

Diane was overjoyed with unworldly love and peace.

Chapter Nine

After the Funeral

The Denari-Gianni clan was exhausted saying their goodbyes to the last of the mourners. Gabrielle invited all of them to come over. She hired a caterer so they could be together before heading back to their lives.

Everyone was grateful for the time to just be with family and relax. Their usual boisterous family was very quiet and subdued. Grief was exhausting.

Jax and Kathleen went outside in the back yard to spend some alone time. Kathleen gave him so much strength and they were so in love. They both tried to date others, as they met so young, but their hearts belonged to one another. Jax understood how his dad felt about Diane. The heart wants what it wants.

Gabrielle asked Diane when she and Luca would be leaving the next day. Diane told her they had an evening flight. Gabrielle seemed very pensive and asked Diane if just the two of them could meet for lunch the next day at Pomodoro's. Diane was taken by surprise but agreed. Gabrielle said she would make reservations at noon if that would work. Diane said she loved that restaurant and would see her at noon but was curious about her invitation.

Gabrielle was waiting at a table when Diane arrived. Gabrielle was drinking wine but when the waiter came Diane decided on black iced tea. The waiter apologized and said there would be a forty-five-minute wait. Gabrielle was glad to have time uninterrupted.

Gabrielle was having trouble making eye contact with Diane, which was so unlike this confident, poised woman. Tender hearted as Diane was, she took one of Gabrielle's hands, looked in her eyes, and asked what was wrong. The words tumbled out of Gabrielle so fast, and she was crying, so it was hard to even understand her.

Diane said, "Gabrielle, please start over. We are family and you are safe with me."

Gabrielle said, "Diane, I knew from the beginning that you would always be the one for Jesse. He was always honest about that, but we both thought we could make it work and I wanted Jax to have a father.

"We had mutual respect for one another and when the invitation came to your friends' Bradley and Cyrena's wedding, I thought it would be a way of closure to end things with both of you. I even encouraged Jesse to go.

"It didn't work like I planned, and Jesse was so sad and distracted when he came home. When I kept asking him what the matter was, he finally told me he wanted a divorce. He just couldn't go on without you.

"Diane, I surprised even myself with my reaction. I told him that there would be no divorce and if he followed through, I would turn Jax against him. I even used the word hate. We got in a huge fight and Jesse slept in the guest room.

"It's my fault that he was sick all the time, and yet I did nothing. I worked healing enough soldiers in my practice in Vietnam to know what a broken heart looked like. Now I will have to live the rest of my life in shame for what I took from both of you."

Diane was very still and sad that they could have shared some happy years together as she was still single at the wedding. She was quiet for a few minutes and then spoke.

"My dear sister-in-law, I have always admired your beauty and how you overcame what happened to your family in Vietnam. You have healed so many people in your career and you saved Jesse and gave him the best gift, which is your son. You have been an amazing mother to Jax, and I am truly sorry for the part I played in your marriage."

Diane could hear the words that she spoke to Jesse in her mind so many times and spoke them out loud to Gabrielle, "God always has a plan, and his plan for me was Luca and my children that I love with all my heart. Jesse and I never fully understood what we felt for one another. It was as if we were two parts of a whole, knitted together with one heart by some strong force. I am deeply sorry for the pain we both caused as you deserve to be number one to a good man, and I hope you can find it with someone."

Both women felt like years of weights were lifted off their shoulders and Diane lightened the mood and said, "It appears our children will be having a wedding soon by the looks of things. It's wonderful they can have their two mothers to join in their blessings and give them wedding suggestions they probably won't want." They both laughed at the image of that thought.

When they finished their amazing meal, they hugged outside a very long time, finding comfort in grieving the same man. They would honor Jesse's memories by loving each other.

Yes, it's so true. God always has a plan.

Chapter Ten

A Time to Mourn

*When we are no longer able to change a situation,
we are challenged to change ourselves!*
-Victor Frankl

Jax after the funeral

I am just standing in the family room staring at my father's favorite chair. It was his worn-out recliner and everyone that came to visit would tease him about it looking worse than the chair the character Marty had in the television show *Frasier*. He would grin, but liked it just the way it was, and our dog Rocco liked to snooze on the floor next to him.

Rocco was standing next to me now and started whimpering. We both stared at the chair as though Dad would materialize out of thin air. Rocco started moping around the house since the day my father was admitted to the hospital. "I know buddy, it's hard, isn't it?" I said, petting the top of his head.

My mother grieved in her own quiet way. Whatever Aunt Diane said to her when they went to lunch before she flew back home with Luca, seemed to give my mother great peace. I know Aunt Diane had her own share of grief to process. She was a great comfort to me and Uncle David at the hospital that last day. Truthfully, I think my father waited for her to come before he passed.

I can't even imagine what my mother went through when her whole family was killed during a church service in Vietnam, which makes me admire her even more. I always wondered how she found the strength to go on. I guess my mother is a survivor and I pray I can be a comfort to her in the coming days.

I will always be grateful to her for helping my dad in Vietnam. Uncle David said Dad was pretty messed up and being a combat soldier was like a trip in hell. It was especially hard for him losing his closest friends, especially Ben, but other than that he never wanted to talk about it.

Mom told me one day that my father kept in close touch with Ben's widow. He sent Ben's children birthday and Christmas cards and attended both of his sons' college graduations in Indiana. They in turn were all three at my father's funeral with broken hearts for the man they came to love and a link to her husband and their father's past, knowing he was there when he died.

A broken heart is an awful thing to experience. I read that the more you love the more you grieve. Was it Tolstoy that said that? I couldn't remember.

Grief is something people deal with every day. In my experience grief is like walking near the ocean shore and feeling like everything is fine. Then out of nowhere a big wave comes and knocks you off center. And the cycle keeps repeating itself, again and again.

A month later my mother asked if it would be too hard for me to clear out my father's room. I said "of course, no problem." I would do anything to lessen her burden even though the idea filled me with dread.

My parents quit sharing a bedroom after the big fight they had when dad returned from his friend's wedding. Nothing was ever the same after that night. It no longer felt like a happy home to me.

I now understand that Diane was the only true love of his life, and that had to be a bitter pill for my mother to swallow. The heart seems to have a mind of its own, and I understand how hard he tried for my sake to make it work with my mother. It had to be very painful for her, knowing she would always be second choice.

My mother is an extremely beautiful woman, turning heads wherever she goes, but beauty sometimes isn't enough. I am forever grateful to her for sacrificing so much on my behalf.

I went to my father's room that I hadn't entered since the day the ambulance picked him up and took him to the hospital. The same linens were still on the bed, and I held his pillow, breathed in his scent and then I totally broke down.

I started with his closet first. I phoned his brothers, David and Luca, to see if they wanted anything. Uncle Luca was the first to respond. "No buddy, I have all the memories of my brother tucked safely in my heart." Uncle David tried to put some humor into it. "There is no way I would want all the Seattle sports hats and sweatshirts he wore." Dad and Uncle David loved that sort of banter. Being from the Midwest they constantly bickered over their favorite teams. They were hilarious but it was always in good fun.

So, I put everything neatly in boxes to give to charity. It's very emotional to give away a loved one's belongings because you are acknowledging that they will never be back, even though logically you know it to be true.

In the very back of one of the drawers I saw a shiny object. I almost missed it but when I reached my hand far back inside, I saw that it was a very beautiful diamond engagement ring. I was pretty sure who that ring was bought for, and sad that dad kept it and probably never lost hope to have a life with Diane.

I will have to ask Uncle David and Aunt Darla what to do with it. It would be in poor taste to ask anyone else, and I would never let my mother see it.

There was a box in the next drawer that held his Purple Heart with other medals given to him from the war. It bunched up in the middle with satin material. Underneath was a stack of letters from Diane that he had kept all these years. It broke my heart realizing the depth of love a young Diane felt for the soldier Jesse.

He must have told her in person about my mother because there were no letters to indicate otherwise. Aunt Diane was empathic even back then because of one of the letters that was dated April 7th. She wrote that she had a dream about a beautiful woman with dark hair and felt unnerved all day as to what it meant. I believe she was seeing my mother. My father must have known too when he read it.

They talked about mutual friends dying in Vietnam and Diane would tell him what was going on in the news. They couldn't wait to see each other when he was finally coming home. I can imagine the reunion the two lovers had at the airport. I felt tears flowing down my eyes.

They were counting the days until they could see each other. It was almost eerie at how similar they were to me and Kathleen. "Please God, I prayed, let Kathleen and I be together one day."

My Grandma Kate loved Diane like the daughter she never had. She even passed her family ring down to Diane shortly before her death. But to Grandma's credit, she was always wonderful to my mother. Kate and Steve adored their whole family and would do anything they could for every single one of them.

I took the things that needed to be hidden from my mother and put them safely in my room for now, looked back at the empty room, took a deep breath, and closed the door.

When my mother saw me walking down the steps with the last box, I saw her visibly take a deep breath and her shoulders relax.

"Thanks, my boy," said mom. "I understand how hard that had to be for you and I am so grateful." We were both holding on to each other, crying now and allowing the tears to flow.

The next day I decided to read the book my father and his friends wrote about being in Vietnam. My mother and I were surprised, although very grateful that it was being published. Sergeant Smitty actually called today to tell us the book sales so far were off the charts. He checks up on us from time to time.

My father would have been so pleased and I'm sure the veterans were glad that their voices could be heard through the pages for validation of what they went through. I thought the title my father chose, *Vietnam-A Soldier's Story,* was pretty cool. It was a very large book that was 333 pages long. It had to have taken a lot of gut-wrenching determination for such a huge undertaking to have it ready to publish.

Since my father never really talked about the war I was in for some shocking news, and it was clear that the soldiers knew they were being lied to by the government.

When I was a boy, we took a trip to Washington D.C. We visited the Vietnam Veterans Memorial Wall. It was 7.5 feet high and 375 feet in length, containing more than 58,000 names. It's called *The Wall That Heals* and honors more than three million Americans who served in the U.S. Armed forces in the Vietnam War.

There were people standing in front of the wall crying, some were saluting, and others were very silent after finding the names they were searching for. My father was unusually quiet the rest of the morning after he found the names he recognized.

We went to the park in the afternoon, bought some hot dogs, and watched some people playing softball. My father started to relax, and I will always remember how much I enjoyed doing something so simple with my parents on that sunny afternoon. A baseball game and a hot dog. My kind of day.

I remembered that my Grandfather Steve served in WWII. We were studying about the *Battle of the Bulge* in history class and how the Germans surrendered a few months later. I called and Grandma Kate answered the phone. "Grandma, I have some questions to ask about WWII." She said my grandfather wasn't home, but she would be happy to help me.

Grandma said it was called the *Ardennes Campaign,* but Winston Churchill named it the *Battle of the Bulge.* The men in WWII were known as the greatest generation. "Anyways," said Grandma, "the Ardennes Forest was bitterly cold and eighty-five miles of dense woods. The army had one hundred thousand casualties, but the Germans surrendered less than four months later. Your grandfather met famous generals, one being General Patton."

"Grandma, I saw a movie about him, and the soldiers nicknamed him *Blood and Guts*."

"Yes!" replied Grandma. "He also met General Bradley. The soldiers loved him, and he was referred to as the GI's General."

"Anything else that might earn me an A, Grandma?"

Grandma continued, "Here is something very impressive and it also is a great lesson on endurance and never giving up. There was a man of small stature named Audie Murphy. He probably only weighed 112 pounds, but he became one of the most decorated American combat soldiers in WWII."

"Thanks Grandma, you've been a lot of help. I love you."

"I love you too, honey," and then we both hung up.

Those memories talking to Grandma feel like a lifetime ago. Never did I dream back then that I would be holding a book in my hands that my father wrote about yet another war.

The book was fascinating, and my father talked about being stationed in a place called *Chu Lai* that is a seaport, in the *Quang Nam* province of Vietnam. The longer the men were there, the more disillusioned they became. Many became addicted to cocaine and heroin, because seeing death every day and wondering if you were next, took a toll on all of them.

The village people were very bright and made handmade booby traps. Guys were getting legs blown off and nobody knew friend from foe.

One day a scout in my father's platoon fell in a camouflaged punji trap. Punji traps are made of bamboo, and sharp and strong as steel. The trap is filled with fresh human and animal excrement causing life threatening infections. My father ran up ahead when he heard the scout scream and saw him ten feet below with a sharp spear penetrating his torso. He retched and almost blacked out at the sight.

He yelled for the medic named Erik, which I met at my father's funeral. Erik gave a tribute to my father at his funeral and had a sweet little girl with him. I could see how these men would form strong bonds from what they endured.

My father lost it when his best friend, Ben, died. After losing several other friends he concluded that he would never leave Vietnam alive. Then he was wounded during a surprise battle from the Viet Cong. He described seeing the dead bodies one on top of each other and the sickening smell of blood from the hot sun. His leg took a hit that knocked him to the ground, and he crawled to the bunker. His boot was filling up with blood and the next thing he remembered was being rescued by a Huey helicopter and taken to the hospital.

There were many things written in the book about a girl named Diane that was the love of his life. When despair overtook him, his chaplain told him to get some help from a French-Vietnamese doctor that helped many soldiers. Mother helped him survive and they developed a close relationship. They had one slip up and I was born from that union.

I finally understood that Diane was really the only one he truly loved, but he was forever grateful to my mother for saving his sanity with her treatments. I believe he loved them both in his own way.

When Diane told him he needed to be with the mother of his child, it forever changed both of their lives.

I felt so proud of the way he described my mother and all the soldiers she helped suffering from PTSD including himself. My father along with my mother are both heroes in their own rights.

Vietnam was a war that should never have happened and when they held protests you could even see vets with purple hearts joining in.

I closed the book and knew it would forever be the most important book I would ever read. It is amazing to me how humans could survive in those conditions. So, I will forever be grateful to have known and loved my father and the impact he made on me as his son.

✳✳✳✳✳

Kathleen

After I got home from Uncle Jesse's funeral I had so many thoughts weighing on my mind. I understood how his son, Jax, felt and tried to comfort him. I felt very sad for Jax that his father died so young. It brought up so many memories of my mam dying when I was young. I knew what a shattered heart felt like.

My mam, Shannon, was madly in love with my father, Liam. He always called her his *grá mo chroí*, which meant love of my heart. He was only in his late twenties when he was killed in Vietnam. He planned on taking us to Ireland where his family lived after the war.

My mother slept next to his framed picture on her nightstand until the day she died. My poor mam, three months, and just like that gone from cancer. One of the last things she said to me was, "Kathleen love, live your dream like you and your da talked about."

My parents were both Irish and Da dreamed about living in the country and being a sheep farmer in Ireland. Da's brother, Shawn, lived in Ireland.

Da was a great storyteller. He always called me his *Bonnie Lassie*, which meant little girl. I would sit on his lap for hours, where he would take me on adventures to the *Emerald Isle*, as he liked to call it, when he was a young boy living in Ireland.

He only lived in America a few years before he was drafted. He missed his family, especially his brother, my Uncle Shawn. Uncle Shawn lived with their mother, Nan Grace, and always kept in close touch. I only met my uncle once, at my da's funeral but remember him being so kind to Mam and me. I loved living on the beach, but his dream of Ireland seemed to be taking a life of its own in me lately, coupled with my mam's last words.

I am so fortunate that my mom's best friend, Diane, and her husband, Luca, adopted me. I love these people with all my heart, and I inherited four brothers that already felt like brothers, before my mom passed. Luca was especially understanding because he was also adopted.

My mam was a talented artist and owned a gift shop on the beach. Our cottage was just a block away from the Gianni family but we both knew Diane before she was married to Luca.

I want to see the world before I settle down. My Momma Diane promised me a trip to Ireland after graduation with my two oldest friends, Fiona and

MacKenzie. Fiona is our funny friend and always makes Kensie and I laugh. Only two weeks until our adventure begins, and we are all so excited!

I am sad to say that we heard bad news about my Nan Grace today. She died. We were both excited to meet face to face for the first time. Gran has been very ill and couldn't travel, so I guess it wasn't meant to be. But we came so close.

A gift from Nan Grace came in the mail from Uncle Shawn. It was a ring worn by her very own mother on her wedding day and she wanted me to have it. I held it in my hand, tried it on and marveled that it was a perfect fit. My Great Nan's name is Bette. The year 1918 was engraved inside. It was called a Claddagh ring and handed down from one generation to next. It was used for wedding ceremonies and was quite beautiful.

The energy on the ring felt like love. My Great Nan Bette was a healer for animals. It was said that she could communicate with them when they were sick to tell her what was wrong.

Uncle Shawn said there will be a *Reading of the Will* when I arrive. I'm not much of a lover of money. I would have rather been given the chance to spend time with my Gran face to face instead of through letters.

I love Jax but I have wanderlust. I'm not quite ready to settle down. There is so much I want to see first in this big, beautiful world!

So many dreams. I pray when the time is right, Jax and I will share a life together.

Momma Diane said it will come; God always has a plan!

Chapter Eleven

Welcome to Ireland

Fáilte roimh Éirinn.

When Kathleen entered the airport after a very smooth flight, she spotted her uncle waving excitedly. He looked so much like her da. The only difference was that he had white silver hair and blue green eyes the color of the sea. She ran over to him, and they hugged each other tightly.

"Welcome to Ireland lass, I am so happy to see you," he said grinning from ear to ear. "Aren't you as pretty as a picture."

"Thank you, Uncle, I am so excited to be here!"

The deep timbre of his voice was exactly how she remembered the voice of her da. His hair would be silver now too, had he lived, she thought sadly.

After they gathered her luggage, he told her they would go straightaway to his house where he had a proper Irish meal waiting for her.

Ireland was so beautiful and more. Vibrant emerald spring grass, rolling hills, winding roads, magnificent eggshell blue skies, and heather along with other wildflowers, seemed to be growing everywhere.

Kathleen watched in awe of the pastoral setting before her to see cows grazing, and purple mountains on the horizon, inhaling the earthy scent of pine. She noticed how deeply she breathed in the country air surroundings. There were many whitewashed cottages overlooking the sea, with huge white-capped waves where everything seemed alive and one with nature.

Up ahead they had to stop because sheep were in the middle of the road. Her uncle got out of the car to guide them off so they could get through. Kathleen thought they were adorable! When he came back to the car, she asked him why the sheep were painted different colors. He explained to her that a permeable bag containing paint is hung underneath the neck of a ram released into a field of ewes for mating. As a ram mounts an ewe, the bag of paint leaves a mark on the back of the ewe. This lets the farmer know which females are ready to be moved to another field.

"That's fascinating," said Kathleen. "This certainly is different than living on the beach in the calm gulf waters in America," she added. Her uncle smiled and nodded.

"When might your friends be visiting?" asked Shawn.

"They are to arrive in two weeks, and we would love you to point out places for us to see," said Kathleen.

"It would be my pleasure, Peata," said Shawn. Kathleen remembered her da calling her peata sometimes and knew it was a term of endearment.

Shawn told Kathleen that they had an appointment in town with a lawyer to go over his mam's *Last Will and Testament* the next day. He also wanted to introduce her to the folks in town, then the men that worked on the ranch, and the people on the neighboring farms. "I want to show off my posh niece," he said with a twinkle in his eyes.

Kathleen was sad that she would not be seeing her Gran before she passed, but glad to spend time getting closer to her uncle. She also wanted to learn about caring for animals and the idea of being a *farm girl* filled her with excitement.

Her uncle's estate was tucked behind a rolling, green hillside. She had no idea her uncle lived in such rich surroundings. She just knew he was a farmer and a man with a kind heart and humility.

When they got out of the car the sweetest Irish Collie came out to greet them. "Mind yerself," said Shawn as he wagged his tail. Kathleen petted him and asked his name. "Clover," replied Shawn. Kathleen loved him already and it looked like the feeling was mutual.

Kathleen was excited to live with her uncle for a whole year in this grand place. The outside was whitewashed with a bright cranberry front door. Her uncle had the most brilliant colors of Irish roses along the front of the house. He carried her luggage from the trunk and opened the front door. "Welcome, welcome," he said. "Come on in lass."

First thing he did was go straight to the kitchen to make her some Lyons tea and explained that it's the Irish way of showing hospitality when someone comes to visit. He then fed her the most amazing Irish stew that she had ever eaten, with some Irish soda bread, until she was stuffed full.

Her uncle then gave her a tour of the house. It had three floors and the third floor had massive halls. He said it's where the help lived in the old times. It had dark wood furniture, cabinets, and marble floors throughout, with many fireplaces, each ornately engraved. There was a music room with a piano, violin, and fiddle where company would come sometimes for fun, to sing, and dance.

She was so touched when he showed her the loveliest room for her to sleep in with a white comforter and matching pillows. He had a vase filled with pink Irish roses that smelled heavenly, and soft pink linens and towels on the dresser.

He even had a fluffy white robe on her bed. Her bathroom had a stained-glass window, and her bedroom overlooked the sea. She had tears from being overcome with gratitude for being made so welcome.

Most of the house had cranberry floral covered wallpapers. There was a pool table in one room and antiques everywhere the eye could see. She knew when she entered her grandmother's room that it belonged to her as she had goosebumps and a feeling of being enveloped in love.

Shawn said, "Aye you can feel the other world lass." Kathleen gave him a soft smile.

Her uncle had the most amazing extensive library-study where he spent his time, with bookshelves holding hundreds of books. A wooden ladder was placed on the side for climbing up to the top. Lastly, the back of the house had a washer and dryer with a few bikes by the door. Shawn told Kathleen he was mostly a gentleman farmer. He added that he left two of his most trusted men, Garrett and Finnegan, to oversee the ranch. Uncle Shawn had training as a veterinarian.

Chapter Twelve

Emerald Isle

Live in the sunshine,
swim in the sea, drink the wild air!

-Ralph Waldo Emerson

When they finished the tour of the house. Shawn asked Kathleen if she wanted to rest. She told her Uncle Shawn that she was too excited and going to go for a walk.

"Enjoy the sights lass, tis a lovely day for a walk," said Shawn.

She felt so much joy bubbling up and couldn't believe she was truly here. The beautiful surroundings were *grand*, as the Irish people liked to say. The lush, green grass was a vibrant color she had never seen before. She took off her shoes to walk in it and it felt like a soft carpet under her feet. Up ahead were cliffs and the sea, and to her right were lambs that were grazing in the fields. She could hear their sounds bleat, bleat, bleat, and was fascinated by them. She never saw a lamb at their beach cottage back home, she smiled to herself.

She started to run to the sea with joy in her heart. She knew what her da felt, telling the stories to her as a child about Ireland. She knew that she was somehow home in her heart. It was hard to explain or put into words, but Ireland was in her blood. When she got to the sea, she spotted a large rock and sat upon it. It was breezy and her hair was tousled from the sea breeze along with her white dress.

She was a most beautiful young woman and so feminine. She watched a family of white ducks and a few colorful boats docked on the shore. She raised her arms up to heaven with the warm sun upon her face. "Oh Da, I wish you could be here."

When she opened her eyes, she saw her da standing there smiling. Surely, she wasn't seeing this, so she rubbed her eyes again, and he was still standing there with his brilliant smile. Then he disappeared, but there in his place was a beautiful rainbow. They say that Ireland is a mystical place and Kathleen now understood that it was true. Da was happy his girl made it home.

After a long while she started back to see if her uncle would like to have some tea and watch the sunset together. They would be leaving first thing in the morning to meet with the lawyer to hear Nan Grace's *Last Will and Testament* read.

Kathleen thought again how sad it was not to spend time with Nan before she passed. She wanted Nan to tell her stories of her da as a boy. She would be sure to ask her uncle to tell her stories about his brother growing up and if they were mischievous like her brothers back home.

When she was almost home, she saw two men watching her. Probably men that worked on her uncle's ranch she thought. One tipped his cowboy hat and the other approached her. He had on a navy shirt, worn jeans and navy wellies on his feet.

"Howeyeh," he said. "My name is Finnegan O'Shea."

"Hello," replied Kathleen. "Nice to meet you."

"Laird, you are from America. Yas need to laryn how to talk our English in the Emerald Isle, or you'll never survive here," he said. In spite of herself, Kathleen started to laugh.

She knew this type of man. He had a mischievous twinkle in his drop dead gorgeous green eyes, the color of the Irish sea. He had a deep husky voice, black wavy hair, chiseled features and was one cocky muscular rugged hunk of trouble.

Growing up with four brothers and male cousins, she totally understood men. She met boys like this at uni and they loved to see girls swoon over them. Kathleen could see right through them.

"Tis a glorious day lass," he said trying to make conversation.

"It is indeed," replied Kathleen. "I must be getting back to my uncle," she said and never gave him another look.

He looked shocked. A total first with a woman.

Finn noticed she was quite lovely with curves in just the right places. A tiny petite little beauty almost looking like an angel in her white dress and long, shiny, dark hair and eyes. He was totally intrigued.

His brother, Garrett, was leaning against the barn with his arms folded across his chest. He could tell from the body language, watching Finn with Shawn's niece that he was striking out. When his brother approached him, Garrett said, "What's the problem boyo, losing your charm?" and chuckled.

Then Garrett added, "Your such an eejit, I told you Shawn said she is spoken for. You be keerful little brother. Watch yeerself."

Finnegan simply replied, "Well, her spoken for man isn't here, and I like a challenge," as he walked away.

Chapter Thirteen

Kathleen Discovers Her Gift as a Healer

Kathleen awoke to her uncle turning on the kitchen light. She hurriedly slipped on her robe to see what was wrong.

"Sorry to disturb you lass. One of our horses is in trouble and I must go to the barn." Kathleen asked if she could go with him, and he told her to get her jacket and boots. Apparently, Garrett and Finn called Shawn for help.

When Shawn and Kathleen arrived, the horse was in severe distress and wouldn't let anyone touch him. He was a magnificent white Connemara pony named Dempsey. Kathleen knew a little about animals but not much, only that they needed love like everyone else.

Her brother, Alon, was always bringing animals home as a boy and now he was a veterinarian like Uncle Shawn. She wished he could be here tonight.

When they walked in the barn, Garrett explained to Shawn that he checked all he was able to but wasn't able to find anything wrong with Dempsey.

Kathleen thought it was pitiful as Dempsey was groaning, making a deep guttural sound. To her amazement she could read Dempsey's thoughts. It was coming through as equine communication with nonverbal cues in the form of confusion, fear, and pain.

It must be the energetic power of the Claddagh ring from her Great Gran Bette that she wore. She heard stories about Bette being a horse woman that communicated with animals so many times before.

Dempsey made eye contact with Kathleen and without a clue what she was doing put a soft fist next to his nose and her other hand on the side of his face. The men were surprised when she spoke softly to the horse and astonished that Dempsey let her touch him.

"Uncle," said Kathleen. "He has mold growing in his ears causing tremendous ear pain."

"How do you know?" asked Shawn.

Kathleen simply said, "Because he just told me."

Dempsey seemed to sense that correct medicine would help now so he gave a sigh, drew in a long breath, and exhaled deeply. He gave Kathleen a nicker sound soft, gentle, and friendly, to let her know they were friends and closed his eyes.

"Sweet dreams Dempsey, you will be all better now," said Kathleen.

The strangest thing was after the men saw the fluid and mold in his ear, it disappeared after Kathleen touched him and said "sweet dreams."

"Kathleen," said Uncle Shawn, "it seems you have special healing powers like your Great Gran Bette."

"How did you heal him, Kathleen?" asked Garrett.

"I just loved him and asked God above to help with the problem. My Momma Diane taught me that love is the greatest healer in the world."

The two men just shook their heads, and everyone went home to get some sleep.

However, Garrett couldn't stop thinking of the whole encounter. He felt something deep in his core being in her presence, and it wasn't just her beauty.

The next morning Kathleen was greeted in the meadow by Finnegan. He was carrying a bouquet of wildflowers and laurel leaves. He held them out to her and said, "Mairnin, these are for you," standing there like an adorable schoolboy.

Finnegan began again, "Do you fancy yeerself some craic. We could go to the pub."

Horrified, Kathleen said, "I don't do any drugs let alone crack."

Finnegan laughed and said, "No lass, craic means fun. Do you fancy some fun?" Now they both laughed and agreed that Kathleen had a lot to learn.

She never even answered him about a date. She thanked him for the beautiful flowers, gave him a kiss on the cheek as though he were ten and couldn't be taken seriously, then walked away.

Finnegan was so rattled that he went to the pub to see if he'd lost his touch. He had plenty of women there to tell him he definitely still had it.

Kathleen called Jax after her encounter with Finnegan thinking they could both have a good laugh about it. Jax was cranky and tired, studying for the last of his exams. Instead of thinking it was funny he got jealous, and they had a blow up. Kathleen didn't even have a chance to tell Jax about Dempsey. She was shocked by his reaction and said they would talk when they were both in a more peaceful mood. They still said "I love you" to each other and hung up.

Ten minutes later Jax called to apologize. He was just tired of being so far away from her. She told him she felt the same way.

Chapter Fourteen

Reading of the Will

When Uncle Shawn and Kathleen arrived in town at the law office an older man approached them. His name was Davey O'Bryan and was a longtime friend of her uncle.

"Davey this is my niece Kathleen," said Shawn.

"Pleased to meet you, Miss," said Mr. O'Bryan.

"The same to you sir," responded Kathleen.

A young woman asked if she could get them a cup of tea, but both declined.

His office had books lined up against the far-right wall and a big cozy fireplace to the left of the room. The mantle held what appeared to Kathleen as family photos taken on vacation. It seemed Mr. O'Bryan had a large, happy family.

His desk was dark oak opposite two posh brown leather chairs where they sat. Their legal documents were in a folder placed on his desk. After a few pleasantries asking Kathleen how she liked Ireland, he proceeded to use a lot of legal terms that Kathleen struggled to understand.

When Davey O'Bryan got to the part of her Gran Grace leaving equal shares of her estate to Uncle Shawn and herself, she thought she heard wrong. Words like vast properties and multi-millionaire were used and she thought she was somehow dreaming.

Apparently, her Great Gran Bette and her husband bought land many years before and passed it down to Gran Grace. Shawn had already drawn up papers stating when he died Kathleen would have what was his, being his only kin--making her a billionaire.

When the papers were signed, Davey congratulated them, and Kathleen was wobbly walking out of the office. Shawn held onto her and said, "Come Peata, let's go to the pub and celebrate. I am most pleased for you, love."

Kathleen held onto her uncle for the longest time, still dazed at what had taken place.

Her father Luca, and Momma are never going to believe this. She couldn't believe it herself.

When she fell asleep that night her Da and Mam came, absolutely glowing with big smiles. They communicated without words saying, "Give back the blessing of being adopted that was given to you Kathleen," and then disappeared. She said a silent prayer that she would do just that.

That's when the idea came to her clear as a bell. "I'm going to open an adoption agency and maybe more," Kathleen said out loud. Her uncle looked stunned when she told him the next day. He thought it was a grand idea!

Chapter Fifteen

Feeding the Hens

Kathleen loved everything about living on the farm.

If anyone could see Kathleen feeding the hens, they would think she was daft, but she adored them and loved their personalities. They seemed to recognize faces.

Garrett was amused watching her one morning and had to smile to himself at the lass. He realized how much he looked forward to seeing her every day, much to his surprise.

"Well good morning girls," said Kathleen. "I have some fruits, vegetables, and berries for you." She learned that they had 30 different clucking sounds and were quite smart.

"Hello, hello girls," Kathleen said in a sing song voice. If Garrett didn't know better, he would have thought the miss drank too much *poitín*, but he knew Shawn didn't have any Irish moonshine in the house.

He recognized that the little beauty was just high on life, dancing around and singing some American tune. He was mesmerized and couldn't take his eyes off of her. Her laughter was infectious.

She was actually carrying a conversation with the hens. They were very comical names. Henrietta, Henny Penny, Princess Lay'a, Hen Solo, Dora-the eggs-plorer, and one that seemed to be her favorite, Matilda, who was quite shy.

She told Finnegan that one day she researched cool names for hens. Of course, his brother was amazed by everything she said and did.

The hens loved when Kathleen brought a reward of meal worms for the wonderful eggs they shared. She noticed the comb on one of the chickens looked pale and added some apple cider vinegar to their drinking water.

"Good day beauties, see you tomorrow, thanks for the lovely eggs," she said, and danced off as she seemed to have music playing in her head. She was actually doing dance steps and Garrett felt the same reaction to her as he did in the barn.

Garrett remembered where he saw that dance before. It was when he went to his cousin's wedding in America. It was called the *Chicken Dance* where people were flopping their arms up and down like Kathleen.

He laughed and realized that she made his day. He made a point to himself that he would call his Aunt Mary Beth that owned a Bed and Breakfast in Florida. It was at her son's wedding where he saw the *Chicken Dance.*

Kathleen noticed when someone put a saddle on Kelpie, he would wince, and his left back leg seemed to drop. A few days before that, he refused to do his jumps. She walked in his stall with a flake of straw, but Kelpie wasn't even interested.

Garrett and Finn said they better have the equine chiropractor take a look. Kelpie seemed apprehensive when the chiropractor used rubber mallets on his spine. He diagnosed his spine as being out of alignment, but Kelpie sadly relapsed the next day. When the chiropractor showed up in the morning, he wouldn't let anyone touch him.

Kelpie kept looking at Kathleen and so she immediately knew it was a sign she was to help him. She kept smoothing her hands over the spot that she felt was blocked. Kathleen believed that he could feel the energy by his expression. After about fifteen minutes Kelpie relaxed and the blockage was gone. Kathleen silently thanked God for guiding her hand as He did so many times before. She also thanked Tanta Gabrielle for teaching her the smoothing technique.

The chiropractor was pleasantly surprised and intrigued at the gift Kathleen was given and spread the news of what he witnessed in the barn.

After that day she was asked to heal many animals on the surrounding farms. She studied many different remedies for various ailments in addition to her healing treatments and thought they went together beautifully. One to move the energy and the other to strengthen the body.

She especially loved being present during the lambings and was positive that adding raspberry foliage to their diets helped with easier and speedier births. She also added a birth aid herb, *Artemis*, followed by two handfuls of ivy fed to the ewes for a good start in life.

Chapter Sixteen

Girls' Vacation

When Irish eyes are smiling, they're
usually up to something.

Uncle Shawn and Kathleen met Fiona and MacKenzie at the airport. They decided to have lunch at a nearby airport pub that Shawn suggested. He gave them last minute directions with a printout of places they might enjoy.

They rented a Volkswagen Golf with a convertible top. Fiona offered to drive because she had been in England recently and felt more comfortable driving on the opposite side of the street. The wind tousled their hair while they sang along with the radio, joyful and excited.

Dublin was the first of the cities to visit and the famous Trinity College established in 1555 was their first stop. It housed over 200,000 books. Monks lived there many years before and the energy left them speechless, along with the Book of Kells, which were four Gospels of Christian scriptures. They were elaborately decorated illustrations of great masterpieces, which left them in amazement.

The next day they decided to start out in Kilcullen's, County Sligo that had a surf vibe where they could chill out. They wanted to experience the seaweed baths that turned out to be heavenly. They even bought organic seaweed skincare products. Kathleen had them ship some to Momma Diane as a thank you for sending her on this fabulous vacation as a graduation gift. She still didn't see the perfect gift for her father, Luca, yet. Same with Jax. She would know it when she saw it. They also went to St. Patrick's Cathedral, which left them awestruck. They had lunch at the Temple Bar Pub and couldn't rave enough about the food in Ireland. The Irish took pride in preparing fresh food. Kathleen ordered *calcannon* which was mashed potatoes mixed with spinach, kale, and leeks. Mackenzie ordered *boxty* which is hash browns and pancakes mixed together. Fiona ordered fish and chips and said it was the best she had ever had. For dessert they were adventurous and ordered Carrageen pudding made with red seaweed that actually was quite good. They ordered Irish coffee as all the carbs were making them sleepy.

Afterward, they went shopping for souvenirs on Grafton Street that had the most fashionable shops in the city. Kathleen bought some Tullamore D.E.W. for her Uncle Shawn, as it was supposed to be the most popular whiskey.

They also toured the Guinness storehouse which was interesting. Some words they kept hearing were *slagging*, which meant teasing someone good naturedly. People asked for a pint of the *black stuff* which meant Guinness. A pint usually meant three. *The Jacks* meant the toilet. They were learning.

Galway was a university town with art, and the music capital of the world. It had quaint, cobblestone streets with music and dancing in all the pubs. The people in the pubs were a warm and fun-loving bunch.

Mackenzie told the girls she had a secret and couldn't wait any longer to share. The three always had secrets but this felt like a big one.

"I'm in love," she began, "with Dylan."

"Dylan who?" they both asked at the same time.

"Dylan Gianni, your brother, Kathleen."

Kathleen knew her brother always had a crush on her, so she was thrill-ed. "Drinks on me," Kathleen said. "Oh, sista sista sláinte!" Hoping something good would come from this, fingers crossed.

They also spent a day at the Blarney Castle that had many steep narrow steps. Kathleen and MacKenzie took a turn kissing the Blarney Stone. Legend had it when you kiss it you will be given the gift of eloquence. Fiona, the wittiest of the three, said it sounded like a bunch of blarney to her. She didn't join in leaning backwards to hold on to the iron rail and kiss it either.

Kathleen always had a special thing for lighthouses for as long as she could remember, so they took a trip to the Hook Peninsula that lies on the southern tip of County Wexford, where the lighthouse is a feature of the remote area. The misty morning with the waves crashing on the shore in front of the lighthouse left them astounded by the beauty they witnessed.

Lastly, they went kayaking in Dingle Harbor. Dingle had many Irish speaking villages with mysterious islands and waterfalls. They visited *O'Sullivan's Courthouse Pub* where *Star Wars* was filmed.

They loved Dingle and picked berries the next morning. Fiona had the giggles and the girls asked her what was so funny, thinking she was going to tell them one of her dumb jokes, and that's just what she did. "You two are a couple of dingleberries." And for some reason that made them all go into laughing fits. Kathleen thought Finnegan and Fiona would make a perfect couple and would introduce them when they drove back to the farm.

Their trip was going by so fast, but these were some of their favorite spots.

There were still many castles to explore and forests and mountains to hike. They promised they would do this again one day and raised a glass to Ireland. Sláinte!

When they got to the main dirt road leading to the farm, there weren't any cars, so Fiona was driving back American style--on the wrong side of the road.

Finn came running out of nowhere. He told her to roll down the window.

"What is it?" asked Fiona.

Finnegan tried to respond without an accent saying, "You're driving on the wrong side of the road."

"Excuse me?" said Fiona.

To which Finnegan replied in his normal voice, "It's the wrong soid of the road ye was drovin down, innit?"

Fiona looked at Kathleen sitting next to her and said, "Is this guy for real?"

Kathleen was laughing so hard by now and thought to herself, *yep, I'm going to set these two up for sure. A match made in heaven.*

Chapter Seventeen

Conflicted Crush

The sayings of the wise are like the sharp sticks
that shepherds use to guide sheep.

-African proverb

Garrett found Kathleen one morning in the meadow watching the sheep. He waved and she smiled and waved back. Would he ever get used to the sight of her and what she did to make his heart race?

Kathleen spoke first, "Isn't it the most glorious day Garrett?"

"That it is, miss," he replied with a big smile playing on his lips. She turned him into mush standing next to her.

His good looks didn't go unnoticed by her either. Before he saw her, he was wiping some sweat off his forehead with his shirt which exposed his firm muscles underneath. Kathleen was so happy Jax was coming to visit on spring break from school because this was causing thoughts that she shouldn't be thinking.

"I am having the best day," said Kathleen with a twinkle in her eyes. "I planted a beautiful garden for Uncle. The flowers looked like they were glowing in the sun, and when I finished, a soft rain watered them, as if God above was planting them with me."

She excitedly continued on to tell him that she planted bluebells, asters, buttercups, yellow primrose, and jasmine. She looked up at him and said, "I'm so sorry I must be boring you to tears rambling on and on."

"That could never happen," he said before thinking.

They both looked at each other longer than was proper. Kathleen changed the subject and said she noticed the ways in which ewes interacted with their young. He was amazed at what she knew instinctively.

"Kathleen, the female sheep are very maternal and recognize their lamb's call (bleat) when they wander too far away. They display emotions by the position of their ears and are very intelligent. They also recognize emotions by facial expressions and self-medicate by eating certain plants that can cure them.

"They have a great sense of smell and special scent glands located in front of their eyes. Mothers learn to identify their babies by their unique scent."

"Fascinating," said Kathleen as one baby lamb came right up beside her.

"You are a healer, Miss, and the animals are able to connect to your life force of love. It's a gift given to certain people and should be respected as the Creator gifted it. Shawn said your Great Gran Bette had that same gift and used it on people as well.

"If you want to join me and observe my equine assisted psychotherapy sessions, I think you would be grand. Essie McKenna was the towns' healer that recently passed at age 96. They would be blessed by you, of that, I am sure. Most of the folks in these parts always choose natural ways first."

Kathleen was speechless and the words of Tante Gabrielle came back to her saying she believed that one day God would use her as a healer to help others.

"Thank you, Garrett. I will take to heart what you have said to me and call my Tante Gabrielle, who shared some of the same words you said to me many times." At that, she wished him a lovely evening and walked off with many thoughts swirling in her head.

✱✱✱✱✱

Garrett

I invited Kathleen to go on a picnic with me to thank her for all the help with the animals and sharing her gift of healing. A whole year gone by so fast. The weather would soon be turning cold with winter upon us. My brother Finnegan wanted to come but I told him next time.

My brother gave up on Kathleen when he realized she thought of him like one of her brothers and grew to love her as a sister. He was teaching her how to talk like an Irish woman and somedays they were doubled over with laughter. "What's dotey love?" asked Finn. "I forgot," said Kathleen. "It means cute, adorable or smitten," said Finn and on and on they would go to the next word. Finnegan was proud to say that Kathleen was developing an Irish lilt to her words.

Sadly, I did not think of her as a sister but never told her how I felt. What was the point as she had the man she would marry waiting for her? Should

I just tell her anyway what I thought about to myself?

There were certain times that I thought she might feel something for me too. Sometimes we seemed to both make prolonged eye contact and had to both look away. Maybe it was just wishful thinking.

The lass had a sparkle that lit up a room and big brown eyes the color of warm liquid honey. A man could get lost in those eyes. I have never felt this way about a woman. She's an absolute stunner!

She loves working on the farm and will do any job asked of her. Animals gravitate toward her, and she even has a young lamb that follows her everywhere lately. She affectionately named her Mary, after the children's nursery rhyme.

The lass is filled with love for all of creation which has to come from God. She is by far the most compassionate soul I have ever met. When I spend time with her, I feel like I am home, which is a new feeling for me that I have never experienced before. She is a very gifted healer but credits God for all of it. When she gets called into town to help someone, she always makes time.

One evening I walked to the shore at the golden hour and there she was, such a vision of beauty it took my breath away. She spotted me and waved me over.

"Evening lass, tis a lovely sunset we will be having shortly."

"Oí che mhaith," replied Kathleen with a radiant smile.

Garrett smiled. He couldn't seem to stop grinning around her. It was embarrassing. She was saying good night but that was close enough. He would leave her schooling to Finn.

"Please stay and watch with me," said Kathleen.

They were so peaceful sitting side by side, watching the heavenly sunset changing colors in golds and pinks while the sound of the waves rocked back and forth creating a rhythmic soothing balm to their hearts.

Kathleen said, "My mother used to watch the sunsets with me when I was young, and we lived in the beach cottage together. Not sure of all the words but she would read from the *Psalms*."

It was all I could do not to touch her. I thought to myself *oh mo stóirín*, my little darling.

Kathleen went on to say her favorite parts. *"Look at the splendor of your skies, your creative genius glowing in the heavens. When I gaze at your moon and your stars, mounted like jewels in their settings, I know you are the fascinating artist who fashioned it all."*

"Aye the *Psalms*, sunrise brilliance and sunset beauty both take turns singing their songs of joy to you," said Garrett.

Kathleen looked deep in his soulful green eyes, the color of the sea. She was always aware of his handsome looks and powerful body much like his brother Finnegan, but Garrett was more intense and serious minded.

"You know the *Psalms*," she said softly, but they just gazed into each other's eyes, and neither could look away. He took a lock of her hair that was blowing in her eyes and pushed it behind her ear. They both felt the attraction and spark. They seemed to be mesmerized with one another.

Kathleen was the first to stop and abruptly said she needed to get back to

Uncle Shawn. She practically ran all the way back leaving Garrett dazed.

She reprimanded herself. "What are you doing?" she spoke aloud. "You love Jax. What are you thinking?"

She was thinking she was in trouble to be so confused about another man. She was also glad she would be going home to Jax soon and told herself maybe she was just lonely.

Chapter Eighteen

Sláinte!

Kathleen

The folks gathered together every month at the hall which they called the *halla* and filled it with love and fun which they called *craic*. The women brought food, and of course there was always plenty to drink, after all they were Irish.

Kathleen had become quite an Irish cook now, having learned from her friend Mauve, which pleased her uncle greatly. He loved all the home cooked meals but not as much as he loved his niece.

There were a lot of "I'm happy ta see ye, hallo lovely and don't ye look *breá*," which means handsome. The farmers and town folk were warm people that were like one family and always there for one another. And Kathleen was one of them now. They comforted each other at wakes, and rejoiced at births, where the women would crochet little blankets for the wee ones. They were also there to lend a hand at weddings whether it was posh or simple.

One of the farmers, Paddy, performed the traditional *sean-nós*. It was said that he had the smoothest velvety voice in all of "Ar'land." He sang an old-style Irish love song with his dark shiny eyes filled with love looking at his beautiful wife. It was sung like a story. "It's of you I am thinking while I lie asleep. My love and my first treasure." Paddy and Bridget were married thirty years with five children, but it was a love that stood the test of time.

Irish songs are filled with such romance and emotion. Everyone was quiet taking in the beautiful tender words that could be felt in the heart and soul. Then came the loud applause and everyone was up on their feet dancing and singing while the fiddle and flute weaved songs around the joy of being alive.

Mauve came over to Kathleen later and asked if there might be something going on between her and Garrett. "It was obvious when Aiden sang the love song in the middle of the evening about the dark-haired lass in the glen, that Garrett couldn't take his eyes off you," said Mauve. Kathleen responded that Mauve must be mistaken. She felt it too but never looked his way.

Chapter Nineteen

Picnic

*We don't meet people by accident. There is
always reason, a blessing, or a lesson.*

-The Inner Life

Kathleen

I can hardly believe that I've been in Ireland for a year. Jax will be graduating with his MBA, so it's time to move on and make plans for our future. I have made so many friends with the neighboring farmers and the kind folks in town. I will always miss the passion and zest of the Irish people, their sense of fun and how they enjoy life. And boy can they drink and cuss!

Their loyalty and ability to take care of each other is a beautiful thing to witness. I am not sure how I can ever thank Uncle Shawn for opening up his heart and home to me. He has taught me so much, along with all the people at the ranch.

Garrett asked me to go on a picnic my last afternoon here and I accepted. He said to just bring myself and he would take care of everything.

It was one of those beautiful, sunny days where you felt that nothing could ever go wrong. He picked me up in his Jeep and we drove to a lake nearby that was quite lovely. He told me he lived in a small house nearby with Finnegan. He brought a blanket that he placed on the soft, cool, green grass with a picnic basket. He brought me a bouquet of daisies that touched my heart. Inside the basket was hummus as a dip with celery, cucumber, and carrots. He also had Irish Picnic Pie that he made himself, along with strawberries.

He asked me to choose between Guinness or dry red wine. I said I choose both and he laughed. An hour later I realized that I may have drunk too much alcohol and started to feel a little woozy.

Out of nowhere a storm came fast and furious. We ran to a barn that was nearby. The rain came down hard and flooded the roads leading back home. It felt like the roof of the barn would cave in, the way the wind was howling.

We would have to stay put, and Garrett was able to contact Uncle Shawn that I was safe and that he would look after me. We wouldn't be leaving anytime soon but I always felt safe with Garrett. I was shivering from the cold, and he held me to keep me warm as we found some hay to sit on. I felt a stirring in my heart but ignored it.

He seemed sad that I would be leaving. I grew to learn his unspoken words. I would also miss this incredible human being. I was growing sleepy from the alcohol, and he offered his shoulder to rest my head.

We both must have dozed off. When we woke up, he put his arm around me and the raw look of love in those sea green eyes couldn't be mistaken.

He leaned in to kiss my lips, and God forgive me, but I wanted to kiss him back.

I recovered first and told him that I planned to be married to Jax, and that I gave my heart away a long time ago. He said he was sorry, not for wanting to kiss me, but giving it a try anyway.

"How about taking a run for my house, and I can build a fire for us there until the roads clear?" asked Garrett. I agreed against my better judgment.

He had a whitewashed house very close to the barn with a thatched roof and bright red door. There were window boxes in the front with ivy and vibrant red geraniums. It was charming and quite cozy inside.

He put the kettle on to make a cuppa tea for both of us. He handed me some warm clothes to put on and started the fire. He was a very tall man so his button-down shirt would be all I needed. We were very quiet, deep in thought drinking our tea. It was bittersweet for both of us to part company. There was definitely an electrical charge between us.

Garrett spoke first. "You have to know how I feel Kathleen. I have fallen hard for you this year. Watching you do healings and seeing supernatural things together with one mystical experience after another, has been incredible. I never met someone with your big, beautiful heart and just wanted to say my peace."

She looked deep into those soulful dreamy eyes and felt undone. Passion overtook her and she kissed him hard with little resistance on his part.

The alcohol was wearing off and she was filled with shame for her actions and stopped.

"Please forgive me Garrett. I had no right to do that. I will never forget you either and our time together, especially with the animals."

He said he understood but they both knew that wasn't true.

✷✷✷✷✷

Shawn and Kathleen

Kathleen sheepishly walked through the front door after being with Garrett. Shawn immediately knew something was wrong with his niece, as she looked dazed and upset.

"Whatever is the problem love? Sit down and I will make you a cuppa tea and then you can tell me all about it."

When he came back with the two cups of tea and shortbread cookies just out of the oven, they sat side by side, but she was hesitant on where to start.

"The cookies smell amazing," she said. Her uncle knew they were her favorite cookies.

"Uncle, I have made a mess out of my life today. I was shivering from the rain and when we got to shelter, Garrett put his arm around me to warm me up and we dozed off. When we awoke, we took a run for his house to warm up and get some dry clothes. He went to his bedroom to get me some clothes to change into, and I took them to the bathroom while he went to the kitchen to turn on the kettle for tea.

"When I came back, he had a fire started and I felt so warm and safe. We knew we couldn't head back until some of the flooded streets improved. He told me he called you so that you wouldn't worry. Uncle, I may have feelings for this man. What an awful person I am to do this to Jax. I am so confused.

"I was very sleepy from drinking too much wine at the picnic and the added fright from the awful storm."

Kathleen was too embarrassed to say the next part out loud, but when they woke up, Garrett put his arm around her and had an intense raw look of love in his gorgeous green eyes that could not be confused.

Kathleen finished telling her uncle, "He leaned in to kiss my lips and God forgive me, but I wanted to kiss him back. I recovered first and told him I would be marrying Jax. He said he was sorry, not for wanting to kiss me, but sorry for trying."

"Aye, I am not surprised, Peata. I have noticed how he looks at you when you aren't watching, and how you both lean into one another subconsciously when you talk. I have never seen Garrett so smitten."

"It gets worse," Kathleen continued. "He confessed that he was in love with me, and the last year was a mystical experience since both of us see things supernaturally. He said he wanted to say his peace."

"Must have taken a lot of courage for the lad to confess this before you left for America," replied Shawn.

"Uncle, something overcame me when he spoke these words to me and I put my arms around him, kissed him and passion overtook both of us. I stopped and asked him to forgive me and that I had no right to do that. I told him that I will never forget our time together either. What damage have I done? I learned my lesson to not drink so much, that is for certain!"

Her uncle looked deep in her eyes and said "Here is the way I see it love. Sometimes relationships and love can be misguided. I think what you have is a harmless crush for a man you have spent the last year very close to while Jax is far away, focused to finish up his degree. Garrett is an amazing man, but I've seen you with Jax and recognize that it's the forever kind of love you share."

Kathleen took a deep breath and held both of her uncle's hands to her heart. "Uncle, how will I ever be able to leave you? Thank you for comforting me and making me feel better."

✳✳✳✳✳

Garrett

A few months later we had our first light snowfall. I went to check on something in the barn and saw Kathleen and Shawn. She was kissing her uncle on the cheek, and he walked back toward the house. It appeared that they were dressed for church and had returned.

She started to walk toward the meadow and stopped, looking heavenward. Snowflakes were falling softly around her, and she looked *fíorálainn*, what Americans call stunning. She had on a pale blue coat and matching hat with her beautiful long dark hair in curls.

It was hard not to be in wonder and awe looking at this natural beauty, surrounded by nature. I will never forget seeing her like this and will always remember her as the girl that got away.

My most memorable time with Kathleen was when we delivered our first foal together. It was anything but easy. Kathleen cleaned and disinfected the stall, then readied it with straw and extra bedding hay. Orla was ready to give birth as she was in heavy labor. Being a maiden mare, meaning her first-time giving birth, it lasted longer than forty-five minutes which is a sign that she needed help and was in distress.

We had the vet on standby but decided to put a call into his office. We gave her a dose of oxytocin to stimulate her contractions, but it turned into a red bag delivery. The placenta that was velvety and red in appearance was seen first, which wasn't normal. Orla needed help to deliver before her foal suffocated.

The veterinarian came running toward the barn.

Just at that moment Kathleen and I saw a woman standing behind the vet, guiding his hands and out came Orla's newborn. When the emergency seemed to be over, the woman vanished into thin air. We just looked in astonishment at one another. We knew we would remember what she looked like and compare notes later. The vet told me to treat the umbilical cord with an antiseptic solution to prevent infection.

Orla was weak but started to instinctively lick her newborn to remove the remaining membranes.

She was very maternal but when the stallion that impregnated her came to see his newborn, Orla wouldn't let him anywhere near her little filly.

Later on, Kathleen and I asked an artist friend to draw a sketch of the woman we saw. It was confirmed by Kathleen's Uncle Shawn that it was his Gran Bette, the healer of horses. Of course, they named Orla's baby, Bette.

Chapter Twenty

Healer

"To be a healer is to take a step back
and recognize the soul within another."

$\mathscr{K}$athleen had so much to consider and discuss with Jax but wanted to wait until he arrived.

When she was finally able to fall asleep, she saw Tante Gabrielle. It appeared that she was taking things out of her chest and pouring it into Kathleen. She had no idea what that meant so she called her auntie the next day and she answered on the second ring.

"Hello darling, so nice to hear your voice. Jax is so excited to finally come to visit you in person. Are you enjoying your stay in Ireland?"

"Very much Tante Gabrielle, but I have some questions for you." Kathleen went on to tell her about her dream and her auntie immediately understood.

"Are you considering using your gift to heal? Because the dream meant that I was sharing my knowledge and putting it into your heart. Truthfully, I have been waiting for this day and knew it would happen, but first you have to be sure and accept it because it's like signing a contract with God to do

His Will.

He will use you when you are ready." Kathleen responded to her auntie by saying she isn't sure it's a choice. Gabrielle laughed that she understood.

"I will help you all I can, and it would be my honor to mentor you if you'd like. Certain things will start happening to you to prepare your physical body for healing. You may feel a jolt of electricity in your body. Don't be alarmed as your body is changing voltage to heal. It's like changing the wattage of a dim light bulb to a brighter one. You also may experience your hands swelling and going back to normal several times a day. A sunset can bring tears to your eyes at the beauty in nature."

Kathleen sighed and said she had been doing that for quite some time.

"Will that mean you will be wanting to stay in Ireland, sweet girl? I see you have lots to talk about with my son."

"Would you like to fly here with Jax? I could use the support," said Kathleen.

"Of course, if that's what you wish. I will be happy to meet your Uncle Shawn also." They said I love you and goodbyes, then hung up.

Chapter Twenty-one

Jax Coming to Ireland

$\mathcal{K}$athleen jumped out of bed and went to make her uncle a proper Irish breakfast, and then it was off to the barn to feed the horses. Shawn had some business near the airport and said he would be happy to pick up Jax and Tante Gabrielle.

When they all arrived at the farm, Jax saw a girl, in what he would describe as barn clothes, on a hill with sheep everywhere. She had pigtails and looked familiar. She sensed him when he got closer and turned around. She was wearing a yellow t-shirt that said *Kiss Me I'm Irish*. She went running to him and he scooped her up in his arms as she wrapped her legs around his waist. When he finished kissing her senseless, he started to tease her.

"Excuse me miss, have you seen the girl of my dreams. She looks a little like you but more the bikini, surfer, southern girl type?"

"Oh stop, city boy. I will do my best to make a farm boy out of you!"

Just then Finnegan came out of nowhere again as always and introduced himself. Finn always seemed to come out of nowhere. Jax couldn't believe that he was ever jealous. Sure, he was totally handsome, but Kathleen related to him the same way she did her brothers.

"Finn is teaching me how to talk like an Irish girl," Kathleen smiled. Finn spoke up, "Mairnin man, laird this lass is making an auld man out of me trying to say the words right. Then she takes off by herself and I tell her ya canna go alone and ya need to be keerful. She's quite a handful. Nice to meet you Jax," and then proceeded to shake Jax's hand. Kathleen was laughing as she thought Finn was hilarious without even meaning to be.

"Let's go Jax. I want to see my auntie."

"Later Finn," she called out as they ran down the hill. Jax gave her a piggyback ride teasing her that she smelled like a horse.

Tante Gabrielle was waiting by the house with Shawn. She wanted to give the young couple a private moment to say hello.

Uncle Shawn said, "So I understand you want to marry my beautiful niece."

Jax never missed a beat and replied, "Not really sir, I am just marrying her for her money," and the two men laughed.

Kathleen put her arms around her auntie and said, "Come in, and welcome Tante Gabrielle. I am so happy to see you!"

After dinner Kathleen took Jax to the family room to chat. "Jax, now that you understand the enormous inheritance I have received, I need to ask you an enormous question."

"Baby yes!"

"What, I didn't even ask yet."

They went back and forth.

"I know you want to move to Ireland. This place lights you up from the inside. I travel with my job anyway and we've never lived in the same state our whole lives. My home is with you my love, no matter where we live."

Kathleen never loved him more than at this moment. She was going to show him, just when Gabrielle and Shawn entered the room. Jax told them their timing was terrible. They looked puzzled but Kathleen laughed.

Kathleen announced to all three that she planned to open an adoption agency and she and Jax were going to live in Ireland!

Now she would be able to fulfill her dreams of giving back as an adoptive child to bless others.

"Looks like it's happening Da and Mam," she said silently to herself.

Shawn and Gabrielle rejoiced with them!

Chapter Twenty-two

Graduation

$\mathcal{J}$ax was graduating from Wharton at the University of Pennsylvania, and the Denari-Gianni family would all be going to support him. He already had a job lined up with a private equity firm. The family would be driving afterward to celebrate in the Blue Ridge Mountains.

The graduation was great except for one of the speakers. He would have been able to cure insomniacs as he droned on and on. Jax had a whole cheering section as they all hooted and hollered when they called his name.

They took plenty of pictures and were so proud of him earning his MBA degree and all the work and dedication it took. Kathleen took a great candid shot of Gabrielle smiling so proudly at her son as he hugged her with a broad smile, showing his gorgeous dimples. She would make sure to frame that one for her auntie. He ran straight for Kathleen and all the family gathered around them.

He introduced his family to his closest friends from school and then they went to his favorite restaurant to celebrate. It truly was a happy day, but as all their times together, Jax missed his dad, Jesse, and guessed that would probably never change.

$$*\,*\,*\,*\,*$$

Vacation at the Blue Ridge Mountains

It was a family favorite for reunions since his grandparents, Steve and Kate, planned the first one on Thanksgiving so many years ago. The older generation could all feel Jesse with them. How proud he would have been of Jax. They all reminisced about the kids being so young the first time they went to the Carolinas.

They even managed to snag the same cabins they had before. This time David and Darla had the cabin Steve and Kate stayed in, complete with enough groceries for a month. Kate, that loved to cook would have been proud.

Jax chose this destination because he had something very special planned that he'd waited a very long time for.

They did all the same things. White-water rafting, hiking, and fishing were still their favorites. Just as before, only the women went to the art galleries while the men played touch football and made smores. The men still hated shopping and swore they always would.

Their last evening at the cabin before heading home, Jax asked Kathleen to take a walk with him. She noticed him feeling a little nervous all day. Of course, the family all knew the surprise he had for Kathleen, and everyone was excited. Jax looked up to heaven and said, "Wish me luck, Dad."

They started walking and always felt sad to say goodbye, never getting used to it. It was twilight and appeared as though God turned on a light from heaven making the earth glow. It would be getting dark very soon.

There were flowers everywhere which made such a relaxing scene. They noticed the wildflowers, mountain laurel, bright flame azaleas, and violets covering the ground like a purple carpet.

The beauty of the budding trees and the scent of white pine, spruce, and fir perfumed the air as they stood in awe of the mighty oak and majestic maples.

They passed a bridge and stopped to kiss. They moved on and could hear a waterfall in the distance. Hummingbirds, red robins, bluebirds, and chickadees all singing their own sweet melodies.

They climbed the stone stairway to their favorite spot as evening was upon them, hearing the sound of the night cicadas. They never stopped holding hands and felt as though they were in paradise, so much in love. The blue mist from the isoprene in the air gave it a mystical look.

When they came upon the huge rock with their initials on it from many years before, they turned toward one another, gazing into each other's eyes that were filled with light and love under the bright starlit indigo night.

"Oh baby, you remembered," said Kathleen.

"I could never forget. You are the love of my life Kathleen."

They reminisced about standing on this exact spot all those years ago as teens. Kathleen kept trying to show him different planets, but he kept looking at her. She smiled at him, and that was all the encouragement he needed, so he went for it and kissed her. She told him much later that it was her very first kiss and that he soothed all the hurt spots from losing her mother. Some people don't believe in love at first sight but these two did. So did Jesse and Diane, but they didn't have a happy ending together.

They were both feeling euphoric with chemistry and promise. She clung to him, and he kissed her soft lips, slowly and tenderly. He kissed her gently on her forehead and she leaned into him. This man was so deeply in love with this woman.

She put her arms on his broad, strong shoulders and saw pure desire in his eyes. He kissed her deeply and then did something that surprised her.

He bent down on one knee as he kissed her smooth, delicate hand, never taking his eyes off her. He had a small, purple, velvet box and opened it with a beautiful sparkling diamond.

"Kathleen Gianni, you know I fell in love with you as a teen. Would you make me the happiest man in the world and be my wife?"

She was so still that he was afraid she would say no. Her knees turned to liquid. After she collected herself, she softly said "You bet I will, Jax."

They were so excited and went back to the cabin to tell all the family, waiting with big hugs to congratulate them.

The last morning all the cousins were talking about how they played tug of war at the cabin, girls against the boys as kids.

People always left toys behind, and someone left a rope. So Jax, Dylan, Kai, Alon, Brodny, Dakota and Drew went against Kathleen, Danielle, Daphne, and Dena.

The girls spoke up saying to forget it because they are all strong muscled men now compared to those scrawny little boys from the past. So, they agreed to let Diane, Gabrielle and Darla join them thinking they could still win. It was agreed that David and Luca weren't allowed to join in with the boys.

It doesn't pay to be cocky because they were barely trying, and the girls were giving it all they had and won. Some of the guys were laughing so hard they fell on the hard ground howling.

More memories for the Denari-Gianni family. So much love between them and always there for each other in the good times, as well as the hard times. They were so blessed as a big crazy family and knew it.

Jax took Kathleen behind the cabin to say goodbye with a kiss neither would be able to forget anytime soon.

Chapter Twenty-three

Love Is All Around

To Love, Laughter, and Happily Ever After

Bachelor Party

The whole wedding party had arrived in Ireland, excited and ready for fun!

The groomsmen decided to take Jax sky diving for his bachelor's party. The Denari-Gianni clan has always been an adventurous bunch, along with Jax's friends. Kathleen didn't bat an eye as she was used to their shenanigans and wasn't the type to worry.

Her only request was to take it easy at the pub afterward.

His groomsmen were having one toast after another. They were tormenting Jax unmercifully about having video footage of Jax's knees buckling under him before his jump, and were going to show it to Kathleen. Of course, all of them had the same experience, truth be told.

Jax bought all the men Irish whiskey flasks with a tan leather cover, with what else, but *Sláinte* engraved on each one. The men bought Jax a personalized pewter pocket watch, engraved with a shamrock.

They had one heck of a good time and he kept his promise at the pub while the men enjoyed their drinks a little too much. "Sláinte!" they toasted him over and over.

He knew it was time to go home when they started an attempt at an Irish jig while shouting faith and begorrah.

* * * * *

The Bachelorette Party

The women chose a whole different kind of party.

They had massages and facials, then went to get their nails done. They did some shopping, then dined at a posh restaurant and toasted the bride. They were a very close group and were filled with joy for their girl.

Kathleen gave the women beautiful baskets filled with treasures that were elegantly wrapped. They contained pale pink silk pajamas, rose cocoa scented perfume with matching hand cream, and a candle. Each was wrapped with labels that said, *Bride Tribe*.

The women all chipped in and bought Kathleen a cozy, pale gray, angora blanket with the bride and groom's initials and wedding date mono-grammed. They also bought her a pair of Celtic pearl stud earrings.

They toasted the bride with wine and spent the night together in a quaint cottage inn for the evening, reminiscing.

Once in a while, right in the middle of an ordinary life,
love gives us a fairytale.

-Anonymous

The women were all getting ready and enjoying the dreamy music coming from the church. Gabrielle told Kathleen that she was just on the groom's side and rolled her eyes. She said the boys were having way too much fun with the priest, and Jax was so nervous he was soaked through his jacket. This made Kathleen giggle.

Two of Kathleen's friends from uni, Fiona and MacKenzie, were styling her hair and make-up. They were recollecting their adventures in Ireland and how so much had changed since then. All the bridesmaids arrived shortly after and were getting into their dresses.

Her father, Luca, asked to see her for a moment and said he wanted her to have his adopted mother's favorite pin, a beautiful piece filled with gorgeous green emeralds.

"I know my mother would have wanted you to have this, Kathleen."

She put her arms around her father and thanked him. "I will cherish it always father."

He said he would be waiting for her outside.

Since Daphne was playing her violin with the orchestra, she chose her two cousins, Danielle and Little Dena, to be her maids of honor. Little Dena would always be the youngest they all adored.

After Kathleen was given all her gifts from Momma Diane, Gabrielle, and her aunts Darla and Molly, she was ready for her Momma to help her into her gown. Next came the emerald and diamond tiara that Uncle Shawn gave her weeks ago from his mam, Nan Grace, to sew into her veil.

All the girls gathered around, teary, and excited for their girl, and they shared in her joy! She was absolutely gorgeous. Kathleen told the girls they all looked posh in their beautiful emerald dresses and how much she loved each one.

Diane wanted to share a few moments with her daughter. They looked more like sisters. Diane was an elegant beauty in a stunning ivory suit. She began by holding her daughter's hand, "I know you are missing your mam and da today. Shannon was my best friend, and I will be forever honored she chose me to be your momma after she died. I have loved you since I saw you with your mam walking down the beach with your curls blowing every which way in your little bikini. You reached up your little hand to me from your pail filled with sand and gave me your seashell. I fell in love with you on the spot and your mam knew it."

The two embraced and Kathleen told her momma how much she admired and loved her. Then added, "especially raising those four brothers," and they shared a laugh remembering all their mischief.

They could hear the bagpiper which meant the ceremony was ready to start. They opened the door and Luca had the most stunned look on his face seeing his daughter in her wedding gown.

"You look radiant, and I am going to try very hard not to cry. So come now, that boy has been waiting for you forever."

✱✱✱✱✱

The Groom

Jax was a bundle of nerves when he arrived at the church. He took a little walk behind the grounds that followed a tranquil path to a flower garden with violets, jasmine, and woodland florals that seemed to be spilling into the sunlight.

He deeply inhaled the scent of Scots Pine intermingled with peat and the salt sea air. He walked a little further and saw red clover in the meadows in dazzling green grass that sparkled and shimmered in the gentle sea breeze.

Surrounded by breathtaking beauty, he found that he was able to be relaxed and peaceful. He was falling in love with Ireland!

Walking back, he thought about his father Jesse, and wished he could be here to share this day. He wore a kilt to honor his Irish beauty, but when he asked the groomsmen, they said he would be "kilt" by one of them before the day was over if they had to. He had a group of friends and family that were comedians.

Uncle Shawn thought they were hilarious and said he would dress like an Irishman along with the pipers and musicians. The men happily wore traditional black tuxedos.

He was remembering a quote he read from Chaos of Stars:

And I'd choose you.
in a hundred lifetimes,
in any version of reality,
I'd find you and
I would choose you.

Jax would make that vow to Kathleen today in God's house and truly mean every word. He also thought how strange it felt to ask Uncle Luca for his blessings to marry his daughter. Luca became like a second father to him as well as Uncle David after his father died. The only thing Luca said was,

"What took you so long?" and gave him a big hug and shook his hand.

He walked back to the church and put on his jacket. The jasmine boutonniere had a four-leaf clover added over the flower that wasn't on his jacket when he left.

Since nobody had yet arrived besides the florist, and it wasn't there before, he knew in his heart that the added four-leaf clover was a gift from his father, and he was filled with unspeakable elation!

"I did it Dad," he said aloud, "I kept my promise and never gave up on love."

The groomsmen all started to arrive along with Uncle Shawn, Uncle David, and Uncle Luca, soon to be his father-in-law. The groomsmen were carrying their flasks which was a troubling thought. He wasn't sure if he made the best choice for gifts, but they definitely knew how to have fun together.

Father Patrick O'Malley came to check on them. He was telling them that since Irish men were known for getting cold feet on their wedding days, the guests would lock the groom inside to make sure he went through with the ceremony.

This brought out a lot of hooting and cajoling to the groom. Jax was hoping they weren't all going to be drunk by the time the ceremony started. They offered some whiskey to the Padre. He said, "Maybe just a wee bit lads," and the toasting began. "Sláinte!"

When they heard the bagpipe, it was their cue the wedding was ready to begin. The men noticed that Father O'Malley didn't seem to be very steady walking out of the room.

The uncles would be giving lectures to all of them. Jax said a silent prayer, hoped for the best, and walked in line behind the priest.

JUST
MARRIED

Love is like a mirror.
When you love another you become his mirror
and he becomes yours....
And reflecting each other's love you see infinity.
- Leo Buscaglia

Chapter Twenty-four

Wedding ceremony

The church looked magnificent with its high ceiling, whitewashed walls and contrasting dark wooden benches and floor. At the end of each pew were white and blush-colored Irish roses with greenery trailing down, tied with white satin ribbon.

The altar had two large clear vases on either side filled with the same combination. The sun cast a warm glow through the stained-glass windows. It was truly a romantic, soulful Irish setting.

The musicians took their places. Cousin Daphne was going to begin with a violin solo to the song *Be thou My Vision*. The orchestra also had a Gaelic Harp, Irish Uilleann pipes, fiddle, tin whistle, guitar, and male vocalist that was a friend of Jax's from uni.

They played *The Vow, an Irish Celebration, My Lagan Love, Blessing* by Aimee Monique, *McAllister March,* and *Celtic Dawn.* The music of love and romance made the guests feel lighthearted, as though the sounds came straight from heaven above.

The wedding was about to begin. The bagpiper played *Canon in C* while the men followed behind Father O' Malley as he was a little wobbly taking his place with the men at the altar.

The bridesmaids walked in and were so graceful, as though they were float-ing into the church. Their emerald-green dresses were striking with all the white in the room. They carried bouquets of white Irish roses with wild-flowers in their hair. Next came the two flower girls, Michaela and Katylynn. They were the daughters of Kathleen's best childhood friends, Melissa and Meghan, two of her bridesmaids.

The little ones were precious in white silk and tulle dresses with wreaths of violets in their hair. They took their job throwing blush rose petals on the white aisle runners very seriously, counting "one two, one two," aloud as they were shown during the rehearsal. Everyone smiled at these sweet little lovelies.

Luca looked at his daughter that he loved as his own blood. "Are you ready darlin' daughter?" he asked.

"I am, Father, and I thank you for loving me as one of your own." She quickly pinned the beautiful emerald pin onto her beaded purse from Luca's adopted mother and smiled.

"Ready," said Kathleen.

Father and daughter walked down the aisle as *A Thousand Years* was being played. Jax's breath caught when he saw Kathleen, and they never took their eyes off each other, as though no one else was in the church, as she came to the altar with her father.

Kathleen looked like a regal princess. She wore a long mantilla veil trimmed with Irish lace edging, held in place with the emerald and diamond tiara worn by her Nan Grace on her wedding day.

Her great grandmother's Claddagh Ring from 1819 was tucked into an Irish lace handkerchief embroidered with a shamrock for good luck from Aunt Darla. She placed it in a small, white, poshly beaded bridal bag she carried from Aunt Molly, along with the emerald pin.

She carried a bouquet which consisted of white gardenias and jasmine, that smelled heavenly.

Her long hair was pulled back in a chignon. Her dress was a sleeveless v-neck curve hugging sheath, with a fitted lace Victorian bodice. Her diamond earrings, a gift from Gabrielle that her Grandmere gave her to wear on her wedding day, sparkled like the light in her big brown eyes.

Momma Diane gave her the diamond necklace that her Grandma Donna saved for her wedding day on a delicate thin gold chain. She felt so honored to be the bride representing all the women's families she was now a part of.

When Jax first saw Kathleen walk into the church, the tears came as he waited for this woman that he fell in love with from the moment he set eyes on her. She was truly the most beautiful woman he ever met.

When Kathleen first saw her handsome husband waiting for her, she felt a rush of overwhelming love. He looked like a true Irishman standing there.

Her father lifted her veil, kissed her gently on the cheek and placed her hand into Jax's. He whispered to Jax, "I am leaving my Kathleen in your hands to protect now." Jax, too overcome to answer, nodded his head and the two men hugged.

When Jax and Kathleen faced each other to start the ceremony, Father O' Malley started getting hiccups when he began to speak. "We are here today *hiccup* to honor, *hiccup*, love *hiccup*." Kathleen could smell whiskey on his breath and she and Jax both started to giggle.

They knew everyone in the church was praying that the priest could make it through the ceremony, and God answered their prayers. She also noticed her brothers looking down sheepishly.

The priest started again "Sometimes you just know when you've found that special person and each day you know this is the person you belong to forever. And as we witness Jax and Kathleen gaze lovingly into each other's eyes, it's obvious to everyone here they have known for quite some time."

The couple had a surprise for their parents. They turned around facing the parents. Kathleen started first by thanking Gabrielle for the amazing, kind, loving gentleman she and Jesse raised. She also added that she could feel Jesse with them today. Gabrielle was overcome with emotion and started to cry while Diane reached over to hold her hand.

Then it was Jax's turn to thank Luca and Diane for the beautiful, sweet natured woman that was the true love of his life. Now Diane was crying, and Luca was gulping down tears. But they were happy tears and honored that these two would add them to their ceremony.

Next was the Handfasting Celtic tradition dating back 2,000 years. Father O'Malley placed ribbons around the bride and groom's hands while saying their vows of promise and commitment that they agreed to out loud.

They exchanged wedding rings, an emerald and diamond for Kathleen, and a simple gold band for Jax while they smiled tenderly at one another.

The priest prayed the famous *Irish blessing* over the couple.

May the road rise up to meet you,
May the wind be always at your back.
May the sun shine warm upon your face,

May the rains fall soft upon your fields and until we meet again,
May God hold you in the palm of His Hand.

Father O'Malley ended with these kind words, "May God Almighty bless you both forever. My sincere prayer to both of you is that you always bring love home to each other and be one another's guiding light.

"May I now present Jaxon Armand and Kathleen Rose Denari to all of you. Jax, you may kiss your bride."

When the little flower girls heard "kiss," they covered their eyes and giggled.

Jax kissed Kathleen softly on her forehead while they held hands. He put her hand lovingly to his heart, kissed it, and then swept his petite bride up in his arms as they kissed for the first time as man and wife.

The groomsmen where all hooting and the bridesmaids were clapping. The applause in the church was deafening. Kathleen hugged the kindly priest, Jax shook his hand, and they were surrounded by hugs from everyone. A room filled with love and joy. What could make God happier?

The Irish piper played *Give me your Hand* as they walked out of the church at the recessional.

Michaela and Katylynn went running out the door as they knew it was time for everyone to throw rose petals in the air at the bride and groom.

Chapter Twenty-five

Let's Party

Gracing the deep dark wooden bridge going into the reception hall were thousands of blue and purple twinkling fairy lights curving close to the sides, creating a glow in the water.

The inside was decorated in white and silver. The chairs were white, along with the white tablecloths on long rectangular tables. The plates were white edged in silver with silver dinnerware. There were numerous little bouquets in small crystal vases placed on the tables, filled with white Irish roses and large vases filled with tall white orchids by the hors d'oeuvres. The walls continued the theme from the outdoor purple and blue fairy lights. It looked like something out of a dream.

The musicians from the wedding would be playing at the reception. They started the first dance with the bride and groom. They chose to dance to *I Get to Love You* by Rumble. They were so much in love and waited a long time to get to this day. Jax was saying tender words for her ears only and she had tears in her eyes. They kept kissing each other, so blissed out by love.

Diane and Gabrielle were so emotional and happy to see their children all grown up and happy. They were very dedicated mothers that were born for this job.

Next dance was Luca with Kathleen. They chose *The Dance* by Scott Thomas for the father-daughter dance. They shared such a close bond and even more so, both being adopted by families that adored them. They understood how blessed they were. Kathleen had such a special place in his heart, being his only daughter. The next dance was a mother-son dance. Jax wanted to pick the song and he chose *Thank You Mom* by Good Charlotte. Gabrielle cried during most of the song, and Jax kept hugging her and patting her back.

The dancing got under way, and everyone was coming to life. There was a very sweet surprise by Uncle Shawn, Luca, and David in the front row, leading her four brothers Dylan, Kai, Alon, and Brodny, along with cousins Dakota and Drew in the second row. They had been practicing for quite some time as a surprise to the bride and groom. The *ceol* (music) started to play and the *sean nós* (a form of traditional dancing) began, and they danced their hearts out for this young couple. The applause was booming, and the bride and groom ran up to hug these dear men. Kathleen's brothers and male cousins gathered around her with a group hug. How these men all loved Kathleen and all her sisterly advice. There was lots of hand shaking and hugs from the men for Jax.

Kathleen wanted to do the bouquet toss because she was planning a surprise with her brother Dylan. Dylan was in love with her bestie, MacKenzie. So, the women gathered up front while she took a peek behind her to see where MacKenzie was. Dylan winked at his sister, and she gave him a thumbs up. She had practically put the bouquet in Kensie's hands.

MacKenzie turned around with the bouquet and saw Dylan on one knee with a diamond in a black velvet box to propose. The girls were all screaming and giggling, and of course she said yes and gave Dylan a huge hug and kiss. Diane and Gabrielle were both thinking the same thing. Dylan was the spitting image of Jesse. It was almost like Jesse standing there himself.

Next was the dinner with traditional Irish soda bread, corned beef and cabbage, washed down with plenty of Guinness Stout and whiskey. Keeping with tradition, their cake was made with almonds, raisins, cherries, and spice laced with brandy and bourbon. And the bride and groom on the top looked just like Jax and Kathleen.

Her three cousins Danielle, Daphne and Dena all recited a toast together after everyone was served a glass of mead. "Friends and relatives, so fond and dear, tis our greatest pleasure to have you here. When many years this day has passed, fondest memories will always last. So, drink a cup of Irish mead and ask God's blessings in your hour of need. Sláinte!"

Everyone toasted the couple and shouted "kiss, kiss," which they were happy to comply.

Kathleen's friends from town, Enya, Aine, and Mauve sang the Irish folk song *The Rattlin' Bog* while the fiddlers joined in. Rattlin', means splendid.

Ho, ro, the rattlin' bog
The bog down in the valley o
Real bog, the rattlin' bog
The bog down in the valley o

Well in the bog there was a hole
A rare hole and a rattlin' hole
Hole in the bog
And the bog down in the valley o

Ho, ro, the rattlin' bog
The bog down in the valley o
Real bog, the rattlin' bog
The bog down in the valley o

Well in that hole there was a tree
A rare tree and a rattlin' tree
The tree in the hole
And the hole in the bog
And the bog down in the valley o

The bridesmaids were the first to dance in a circle with their shoes off, twirling around faster and faster.

Ho, ro, the rattlin' bog
The bog down in the valley o
Real bog, the rattlin' bog
The bog down in the valley o

On that tree there was a branch
A rare branch and a rattlin' branch
The branch on the tree
And the tree in the hole
And the hole in the bog
And the bog down in the valley o

Ho, ro, the rattlin' bog
The bog down in the valley o
Ho, ro, the rattlin' bog
The bog down in the valley o

Little children were running around sliding on the floors while the older ones tried to steal sips of beer from the table.

On that branch there was a limb
A rare limb and a rattlin' limb
The limb on the branch
And the branch on the tree
And the tree in the hole
And the hole in the bog
And the bog down in the valley o

Ho, ro, the rattlin' bog
The bog down in the valley o
Real bog, the rattlin' bog
The bog down in the valley o

The women sang faster and faster to keep in time with the fiddler's pace. The old women were up now, swaying their hips and keeping beat with their canes.

Well on that limb there was a nest
A rare nest and a rattlin' nest
The nest on the limb
And the limb on the branch
And the branch on the tree
And the tree in the hole
And the hole in the bog
And the bog down in the valley o

Ho, ro, the rattlin' bog
The bog down in the valley o
Real bog, the rattlin' bog
The bog down in the valley o

In that nest there was a bird
A rare bird and a rattlin' bird
The bird in the nest
And the nest on the limb
And the limb on the branch
And the branch on the tree
And the tree in the hole
And the hole in the bog
Down in the valley o

The music went faster yet, and the old men were stomping their feet and remembering their boyhood, when they danced like the young people.

Ho, ro, the rattlin' bog
The bog down in the valley o
Real bog, the rattlin' bog
The bog down in the valley o

In that bird there was an egg
A rare egg and a rattlin' egg
The egg on the bird
And the bird in the nest
And the nest on the limb
And the limb on the branch
And the branch on the tree
And the tree in the hole

And the hole in the bog
And the bog down in the valley o

Ho, ro, the rattlin' bog
The bog down in the valley o
Real bog, the rattlin' bog
The bog down in the valley o

In that egg there was a bird
A rare bird and a rattlin' bird
The bird on the egg
And the egg on the bird
And the bird in the nest
And the nest on the limb
And the limb on the branch
And the branch on the tree
And the tree in the hole
And the hole in the bog
And the bog down in the valley o

Ho, ro, the rattlin' bog
The bog down in the valley o
Real bog, the rattlin' bog
The bog down in the valley o
Real bog, the rattlin' bog
The bog down in the valley o

And on and on it went. Everyone in the room was laughing, singing, and dancing what they thought was a proper Irish jig. And the more they drank the better they thought they danced. It truly was a splendid, *rattlin'* wedding filled with love.

Chapter Twenty-six

Enchanted Wedding Night

La vie en rose

"seeing life through rose colored glasses."

Jax and Kathleen arrived at the hotel, and he carried his wife over the threshold and gently placed her on the bed, never missing a beat kissing. The room was posh and beautiful beyond description, but totally lost on them, as they were so focused on one another.

When they finally looked at their surroundings, it was totally enchanting. It was all arranged as a surprise by their bridesmaids. They had a light blue bulb put in the lamp that gave a soft glow. There were little white twinkle lights placed on the dresser and a vase filled with gardenias. A box of chocolates and champagne was on the nightstand.

On the opposite side of the bed, that they totally missed walking in the room, was a pair of silk boxers for the groom and bikini panties embroidered with Mrs. Denari. Kathleen just knew this was a gift from Aunt Darla, but she would need a little more courage to wear them. They both loved their Auntie. Kathleen and Jax both erupted into fits of laughter.

When they stopped laughing, they looked deeply into each other's eyes and knew their love was the forever kind. They were totally blissed out by one another the entire day.

Kathleen went to the bathroom to change from the beautiful pale blue suit she wore after the wedding for the short trip to the hotel. They had a flight early the next morning. Jax planned a honeymoon trip that was a secret, and nobody gave her hints, except that she was going to love it!

Gabrielle and Diane bought her a chic white silk and lacy negligee when the three went shopping together for her wedding shower. The negligee really accentuated her delicate curves. Kathleen was petite, lithe and graceful, and her dark eyes shone with the love her husband reflected back to her. She let her dark curls fall loosely down her back.

When she opened the door, he couldn't believe what a lucky man he was, to have this beauty that had a smile like sunshine, for his wife. He silently promised himself that he would do everything in his power to protect her.

When she walked out, she thought Jax looked so handsome lying in bed with the sheet around his waist. Such a rugged, muscular man that had chiseled features with a lock of his dark hair falling over one eye.

She snuggled onto his strong, broad shoulder to rest her head. She felt so safe and cherished by this incredible man that had so much love in his heart for everyone.

They shared a toast with champagne and chocolates, and both reminisced about the night they met at the family reunion in the Blue Ridge Mountains, gazing at the majestic stars in the sky. It was Kathleen's first kiss. They were so young and when they kissed it was as if the earth stood still. Their hearts truly recognized one another.

Jax had a surprise for her. Their Grandmother Kate had given a video to his father Jesse to share someday. Gabrielle found it with his important keep-sakes in his office when he died. Kate had taken little video clips of the two of them together. Kathleen had tears in her eyes remembering this loving woman. She put her arms around Jax and felt so divinely loved.

"We knew back then didn't we Jax?"

"We did," he answered.

So here they were, coming together, as God designed. Two hearts beating as one. He would give this girl the world. Gazing into each other's eyes he kissed his wife tenderly as the woman he cherished for so many years.

"I will love you, Jaxon Armand, until the day I die."

"And I will love you, Kathleen Rose, forever, my beautiful Irish Rose."

Jax had a glint in his eye and a smile playing on the corners of his lips with the dimples she loved. Their bodies came alive with rhythm and grace in-stinctively celebrating each other.

"Wife I do believe I will have the luck of the Irish tonight. I also have a few vows to share that couldn't be mentioned in church."

They knew how to have fun together and share laughter as well as sor-row. The way of life. After telling her *the vows*, she giggled, and they held on to each other tight.

Their connection was powerful with desire that shot through their bod-ies. The two shall become one. This is where they belonged. Love in its deepest form. Both hearts open to one another. They kissed deeply and the rest of the world ceased to exist just like the night when they fell in love as kids.

✴✴✴✴✴

All you need is love and a passport.

Kathleen

Jax surprised me with the most amazing honeymoon destination and to a place I would never have guessed. We had the most romantic time.

My husband, I love saying that, and he calls me *wife*. We are a very adventurous couple and saw many incredible sights in beautiful Dubai. Yep, my man took me to Dubai.

We went skiing in the desert, so different from Seattle. The ski resort is indoors with freshly made powder. We also went sand boarding in the desert and even rode on camels. I really didn't want to climb on but glad I did.

There are a plethora of things to do while admiring beautiful Arabic architecture and learning about their history and culture. We have lots of pictures to share back home and met some wonderful people.

We embarked on a hot air balloon ride that soared over the orange radiant desert at sunrise. That was spectacular!

One day we went to an indoor tropical rainforest, swam with dolphins, and even saw the sweetest penguins. Being able to experience these times with the love of my life was amazing.

The food was quite good but we both especially loved *luqaimat* which are hot dumplings and *samboosa* which are hot pastries. We even drank Arabian coffee.

Our marriage is rock solid, and we are able to communicate our feelings and be vulnerable with one another. When he gives me that slow and easy smile, it melts my heart.

Jax is all male and all mine. We are also very playful and flirty with one another. We went for a walk one evening and didn't get very far, as we had to stop and kiss every few steps.

I looked up at him to kiss him and he looked in my eyes and we both felt such incredible passion. "Kathleen," he said quite seriously, "I want you. Now."

That's all it took, as we both ran back to our room.

Our honeymoon is something we will share with our children and grand-children one day. Well at least most of it.

*****

Jax

I was so happy that Kathleen liked my choice of flying to Dubai. Yes, it was incredible, but the best part for me was watching my beautiful bride shine with so much happiness.

I thought about my dad, Jesse, and could really understand the deep love he had for Diane. I am sorry he didn't get his *happily ever after* but will thank God every day for this woman and cherish her all of our lives. I didn't know it was possible to be so happy and in love.

*****

Kathleen

While I was packing my suitcases and getting ready for the long trip back home, Jax came barreling out of the bathroom with his black hair all slicked back talking Spanish. He pretended to play the bongo drums for effect, so I guessed he was imitating *Ricky Ricardo*. He was being silly and started to sing the theme song to the *I Love Lucy* television program.

I love Kathleen and she loves me.
We're as happy as two can be.
Sometimes we quarrel but then,
How we love making up again.
Kathleen kisses like no one can,
She's my misses and I'm her man.
And life is heaven you see,
Cause I love Kathleen,
And she loves me.

Jax can't carry a tune to save his life, so I was bent forward from laughing so hard. We are going to have such fun adventures, my husband and me.

When he finished, I told *Ricky* to get a move on because it's time to go to the airport.

Chapter Twenty-seven

Hope Center

Cousin Drew sent three different drawings and Jax and Kathleen immediately fell in love with the same sketches. They collaborated with the architecture firm where Drew worked to say it was a big go.

The outside was a whitewashed brick. There was also a lot of glass that produced natural light, appearing as a kaleidoscope of colorful hues as the sun moved around in the sky. It was very unique in its design as Drew was an incredibly talented, creative man.

Beautiful flower gardens with a brick walkway led to the main entrance. The building was enormous. The adoption agency would be on the left wing of the building and the children's wing on the right.

The waiting room for the agency had dark, hardwood flooring, white walls, white sofas, and chairs. The only color was the many green plants interspersed around the room. It was striking!

The center of the building had offices for all the different modalities of workers. It was conservative contemporary, and an innovating environment for employees, with lots of glass, letting in natural light to encourage concentration and relaxation. A large cafeteria with natural, organic food was also in the center of the building. The staff working with children would wear white scrubs with a green embroidered *Hope Center, connecting heart to heart,* written on them.

Outside the children's wing was a playground with swings, slides, and hopscotch. There was a volleyball net, basketball court, and baseball field for the older children. Bookshelves and books were plentiful for all the children.

The Seniors in the community volunteered to take the children fishing, coach baseball teams, or whatever way they could help. It really does take a village and no matter what hardships these children faced up to this point, they would be loved and kept safe.

Part of the playground had a garden for the children to plant flowers and herbs, and since they live in Ireland, potatoes. As for now, there would be enough room for 100 children. There was still more land if they needed to expand.

There were different suites for the children to be divided up by age and gender. Soft colors were specifically chosen to soothe.

The nursery had white cradles and rocking chairs. Hand painted murals adorned the walls with giraffes, little gardens, trees and swings with blue skies and big white clouds that gave it a whimsical feel. The walls were painted aqua, pale yellow, peach, lavender, and sky blue in the different rooms. Each crib had a changing table beside it, and soft pastel area rugs covering the dark wood floors.

There would be adjoining rooms with professional psychiatrists on call for children with severe emotional problems and healers to rock and comfort the younger ones. Kathleen wanted to be part of that group. A natural pharmacy was also nearby along with many different branches of medicine to address whatever the children needed.

The halls would have pictures done by the children, art rooms with bright primary colors with fun teachers, and a music room containing all the instruments, which was Kathleen's favorite. She thought music was one of the best healers, especially nature sounds.

Cousin Daphne agreed to come periodically to be the music teacher. Daphne was actually writing music for some famous singers. They also had a room especially for dancers and wished cousin Dena would come. She was an amazing ballerina and traveled the world.

Finnegan and Garrett would pick up the children that would benefit from equine therapy. Ponies had a special way with children.

One of the side entrances had a very large Apache Blessing hanging on the wall with these words:

May the sun bring you new energy by day.
May the moon softly restore you by night.
May the rain wash away your worries.
May the breeze blow new strength into your being.
May you walk gently through the world and know its beauty all the days of
your life.

Hope Center was known around the world as a one-of-a-kind, world class adoption center. And since they were international, she wanted to keep adding love through uplifting artwork from different countries and cultures.

When potential adopted parents walked into the building, they would see a huge plaque of a little girl with her eyes closed and one hand over her heart. The words on the plaque were, *See With Your Heart.*

Chapter Twenty-eight

Airplane Accident

Another busy fun filled week thought Kathleen, but she was really looking forward to Jax flying home.

She went upstairs to her bedroom to get dressed. After getting out of the shower, she turned on the television.

Just as she dressed in a lilac sundress that Jax bought her with her favorite sandals, she heard the local news anchor interrupt with a special report that the flight number Jax was on, crashed.

Aviation officials were working to determine whether there were any survivors in the massive wreckage. They would be giving more information as it became available to them. Stunned by what she heard, Kathleen dropped the bottle of lotion she was starting to apply to her arms.

She went down the stairs like a robot on wooden legs to find Uncle Shawn and Gabrielle. She felt as though she was going to faint. Shawn and Gabrielle were sitting at the table playing cards and when they looked up, they were both alarmed.

"What is it love; you look like you've seen a ghost? Sit down and I will get you some tea," offered Shawn.

Kathleen tried to talk but the words wouldn't come out. The last thing she remembered was hearing the sound of her head hitting the wooden floor.

Gabrielle and Shawn both managed to carry her to the couch when she suddenly opened her eyes.

"Here darling, take a sip of water," said Gabrielle.

Then the words all came tumbling out of Kathleen to a horrified Gabrielle and Shawn. Something didn't add up to Gabrielle. Surely, she would have felt something if Jax had died.

They turned on the news to realize the flight Jax took, did indeed crash. They sat there stunned and felt as though they were living in some kind of nightmare from which they couldn't awaken.

As more information became available, it appeared to have been from an explosive decompression, severing cables that left the pilots with no control. It was definitely a mechanical error.

Sadly, all the passengers but four died and they were all critical.

Oh please God, Kathleen, Gabrielle, and Shawn thought. Let Jax be alive.

✳✳✳✳✳

Jax

I was stunned. I had fallen asleep on the airplane reading a book, and the next thing I know I am on my back in a field. I went to stand up but learned very quickly that my body wouldn't cooperate. I finally managed but was shocked to see my body on the ground, while I stood dumbstruck looking at myself.

I also saw three other people looking at me with horrified expressions, as their bodies were also on the ground beside them. I thought it odd that we could see each other. One of the passengers was a cool guy I sat next to, telling me stories about his career as a comedy writer. After a fun conversation we both decided to take a nap on the long flight home. I read a few more pages in my book and fell asleep.

The two women I saw standing were directly in front of me during the flight. They also stood next to their bodies. I overheard the younger of the two talking about going home to get married during the flight.

Nobody else appeared to be moving at all. There were a few quiet groans and then total silence.

Was I dead, I wondered? Were all four of us dead? My last thought was about Kathleen. I saw a little doll on the ground among the wreckage, with mangled bodies and blood everywhere. Then I mercifully blacked out.

✵✵✵✵✵

Kathleen received a call several hours later that her husband was in a coma in a hospital in Washington. The crash happened fifteen minutes after they took off. She was told there were three other survivors but two of them weren't expected to live. There were 134 people dead.

All the Denari-Gianni clan flew to Seattle to see their cousin, along with the horrified aunties and uncles. Kathleen, Shawn, and Gabrielle took the first flight out. They were in shock and understandably devastated.

Finnegan and Garrett sent their prayers and said they would make sure everything was taken care of at the farm. Although Garrett and Jax would never be close friends they had a mutual respect for one another.

Little did they know that fateful night that Jax wouldn't wake up until four months later. Gabrielle and Kathleen gave him healing treatments and physically exercised his limbs. They would never give up on Jax.

Jax received excellent medical care with the proper fluids, nutrients, and medicine to keep his body as healthy as possible. Luca flew down many times, and the doctors updated him on Jax's case.

Jax seemed to be forgetting the accident and now was traveling through random times of his life. He remembered the first day they brought their family dog, Rocco, home. Then he would be at a basketball game with his dad cheering him on. Cub scouts and camping with random memories of his childhood with no sequence to any of it, swirled in his brain.

He relived the day he met Kathleen and their first kiss. And the joy of his wedding and honeymoon. This memory went around over and over as if it was in a loop. The best day of his life.

Then, he would relive the worst day, watching his father die. He would be in the hospital room with Diane and Uncle David.

✳✳✳✳✳

Jax

I heard my mother and Kathleen talking to the doctor in the hall. He told them that the other three passengers that initially survived the crash had died, and that I was the only one breathing now. They were praying that *when* I woke up and not *if* that my brain would be working. Wow, I must have been in some sort of crash.

I could watch all my family come to see me. They were looking at me on the bed, but I was usually floating above them. Sometimes I would go back to my body, but it was so painful, that I willed myself back out. I could see and hear everything, but my physical eyes wouldn't open.

My wife and my mother were exhausted, but they wouldn't allow one negative thought to enter their minds. I always knew my family loved me, but the Denari-Gianni family came from all over the world, numerous times.

When we were alone in the room, Kathleen shared so many of our private moments. She would cry and tell me to please come back to her. I was trying but unable to. I wanted to hold my wife and take away her pain, but I couldn't move.

Dylan, my cousin, and best friend would always talk about things we did that would get us in big trouble if our parents only knew. He is a university chaplain now and looks exactly like my father. He always ended our visits with a prayer.

Cousin Drew was an architect and kept telling me about *Hope Center* being state-of-the-art amazing. What was *Hope Center*, I thought? Must be a design he was working on. I love this guy.

My cousin Kai, a navy man, came when he had leave and always left me with some off-color jokes. He liked to act like a tough guy, but we all knew he had a heart of gold.

Cousin Daphne was our family musician and now a song writer. She would play new songs she wrote that brought up strong emotions for me. They were that beautiful!

Cousin Danielle was ready to take the bar exam to become a lawyer. She was a pistol and told me about funny cases they were learning about. She had the gift of laughter.

Cousin Dakota was pre-med and the more serious of all of us. He would sit by my bed for hours telling me everything was going to be ok. He was going to be an amazing doctor, very positive and encouraging.

Cousin Alon was a veterinarian and told me about some of the sweet animals they treated. He was a sweetheart of a man. He could always be counted on if anyone needed help.

Our two *baby cousins*, Brodny and Dena, were always cheerful visitors. Brodny was in culinary classes. I used to tease him about all the fishing he did as a boy. Now he could learn to cook it properly.

Dena flew in from Russia. She was a pretty big deal as a prima ballerina, but she would always be our *Little Dena*, and never lose her nickname.

Uncle David, Aunt Darla, and Uncle Shawn came often, and it made me so sad to see them struggling while they whispered how much they loved me. I wanted so much to be able to tell them not to worry.

Luca and Diane were like angels to me every time they walked in the room. Their healing presence was palpable. How blessed I was to be loved this much!

Kathleen kept updating me on what was happening at *Hope Center*. *Why does Hope Center sound so familiar? Wasn't that the place Drew was talking about?*

My mother would read me books and uplifting stories of how powerful God is. I used to hear her cry and tell me to please come back. I wanted to say that I was trying so hard, my eyes just wouldn't open.

Prayers were a very interesting thing to me now. I could actually feel them and knew exactly who was praying at any given time as they sustained and comforted me. I learned that praying for someone may be the purest form of love and biggest gift.

Then it happened. I was no longer at the hospital, but saw a white tunnel that you read about, going very fast. Across the way in what looked like a mirage or steamy mist, I could see my father, Jesse. Next to him were my grandparents, Steve and Kate. I started to walk toward them.

My heart was so full of love, but they told me to stop. "Go back Jax," I heard my father say, "You have so much more you need to accomplish on earth and have not completed God's mission for your life."

"We love you honey" said Grandma Kate. Grandma always called me her honey. "We will have lots of fun when it's your time," chimed in my Grandfather Steve.

Then they filled me with some sort of supernatural love, and I was back in my bed.

I heard my mother tell Kathleen, "Go get the doctor quickly!" And that's when it happened. I opened my eyes without a clue that four months had gone by. The doctor came running in with Kathleen and examined me.

I felt confused and all my brain knew at this point, was exhaustion. My cousin Dylan was standing by the bed, and I thought it was my father. Did I go back to heaven again?

I tried to smile at my wife and mother but not sure if I succeeded. They were crying but I think they were tears of joy.

Why can't I remember how I got here? All the memories I had before seemed to have vanished. My brain felt vacant. I drifted back to sleep.

*"Being deeply loved by someone gives you strength,
while loving someone deeply gives you courage."*

\- Lao Tzu

****

Kathleen

As a psychiatrist, Momma Diane said it's too traumatic for Jax to remember the accident all at once. It would take time and we all need to be patient. The important thing is that he woke up. My momma saved my sanity during this whole ordeal. Her faith in God's plan was the glue that held me together.

The great news is we will be able to bring him back to Ireland soon. I am excited to see that *Hope Center* is nearly finished. I had given it very little thought these past months. Jax was the most important person in my life, and I am beyond grateful that he is coming back to us.

There were many more weeks spent in the hospital, but Jax was improving by leaps and bounds physically. He still couldn't remember what happened, although he remembers being on the plane coming home and a baby doll in a field.

Momma said when a shock to the body and mind is severe, the brain tries to protect the memory from coming back too quickly. Between both mothers and my father Luca, Jax was in excellent hands. We were very fortunate to have so many skilled physicians in our family with different specialties.

Jax was finally stable enough to come home so Momma took a leave of absence from the hospital to give him constant care. We were all concerned that the plane ride home would bring on anxiety, but nothing happened. It would be good to care for him at home in Ireland. Maybe *Hope Center* will bring him joy.

Gabrielle shed many tears for her boy, remembering when her husband, Jesse, was going through PTSD, just with different circumstances. Between the two mothers, he had an amazing chance to heal completely.

Our first night home Jax seemed to be having nightmares but when he woke up, he never remembered his dreams.

Then one day while Momma was asking him some questions, he started having flashbacks. More and more of that horrific day started coming back. He seemed very lucid but started to talk about seeing his father Jesse, and his grandparents, Steve and Kate. We didn't know what to think, but my gut said he probably did.

Every flashback seemed to include a baby doll on a field. The day he made a total breakthrough was remembering that the doll belonged to a marine. The marine was going home to see his newborn baby for the first time. That's when the dam burst, and he remembered all of it.

It took many months of counseling, but he was able to start making peace with what happened. I don't believe you can ever be the same after that experience, but like his father Jesse, I knew he would try his best every single day.

To my joyous surprise, he finally remembered *Hope Center* and that we were looking for a cottage to move into.

Chapter Twenty-nine

Adoption Agency

Everything was falling into place for Jax and Kathleen. They found the perfect spot of land to build on and their parents and family all supported them.

They were even in the process of building a cottage by the sea for the family they hoped to have one day. It turned out to be a Denari-Gianni family affair.

Jax was taking care of the government administrators. An international adoption agency and center for children waiting to be adopted was a huge project.

Diane would use her skills as a psychiatrist. She agreed to take time away from the hospital to counsel pregnant women waiting to give their babies up for adoption.

Uncle David agreed to hire the attorneys and help in any way he could. He would also be able to draw up legal documents for the birth mothers to qualify for financial assistance when placing their child up for adoption.

Kathleen's father, Luca, would interview physicians and agreed to take extended time away from the hospital to get everything organized.

Gabrielle had already found adoption specialists and counselors for their clinic. She also agreed to take time off from the hospital to help however needed.

Cousin Drew, their family architect, was overseeing the details of the building. His creative genius qualities were noticed, and his career was going to be phenomenal.

So as always, the Denari-Gianni family would be creating a state-of-the-art center, making something very special come together to help spread love, one family at a time, heart to heart. Kathleen had plans to make sure all the children on the residential wing would be trained in age-appropriate life skills, so that if they aged out of the system, they would be employable, instead of just thrown out to fend for themselves.

They could also give the option of helping the children that aged out of the system a chance to stay and train them to counsel the younger ones. They would make sure every child felt safe, loved, and respected every day. That was their pledge.

Momma and Gabrielle both agree these children were God's design for Kathleen to shine. Her gift as a healer could help these young people heal the scars that were carried in them through no fault of their own. They both agreed that Kathleen had enough love in her to heal the world.

Gabrielle said most of healing is an art and the compassion to heal another soul. She added that Kathleen already had that--times a thousand.

*****

Settling into married life

Hope Center was ahead of schedule and watching their dreams come true was yet another adventure for this young couple. Everyone in town and the farmers were so grateful and thankful for their selfless service.

Jax was still traveling while Kathleen was gaining more skills as a healer along with the rest of the class. Gabrielle really shined as a teacher and she and Shawn seemed to be getting closer, which pleased the whole Denari-Gianni family.

Kathleen completed her Master's in Social Work and all the family, which were spread around the world came to celebrate. Of course, family included Finnegan and Fiona who were there to cheer her on. Finn proposed to Fiona, and she accepted, so there would be a fun wedding to plan in the future. They were so good for each other.

Kathleen called Jax to tell him she ordered some picnic style tables for the children in the group home. She planned on making it festive with colorful tablecloths and tea lights along the walls. The children could decide what they wanted on the walls, perhaps their paintings from art class.

Jax loved hearing the excitement in his wife's voice every time there was another step completed at *Hope Center*. They both agreed that their lives were what dreams were made of.

Chapter Thirty

Children at Group Homes

Let us reach out to children.
Let us do whatever we can to support their fight
to rise above their pain and suffering.
-Nelson Mandela

It was amazing how fast *Hope Center* grew. As an international adoption agency, it drew children from all over the world and potential adoptive parents.

The staff at the center had stellar recommendations and were hand-picked by the Denari-Gianni professionals. The family spent countless hours making sure they found the best in their fields.

Many of the children were eligible for adoption because their birth parents were unable to care for them due to financial, legal, or emotional issues.

Some were beaten and abused from alcoholic or drug addicted parents. And some gave a gift to parents that couldn't give birth. These were the heroes to Jax and Kathleen. They knew for whatever reason, mostly too young or unmarried, that their child could have a better life elsewhere.

In between business trips, Jax was a huge help to Kathleen and helped her get the children situated in their rooms. She even found him one evening rocking one of the babies with so much tenderness. She knew then that he would make the most amazing father.

The first woman to enter the adoption agency was a sixteen-year-old mother that came with the baby's father. They knew they had nothing to offer a child at this stage in their lives. They were given a case worker to make sure of their decision. When the baby was born the birth father's mother decided to raise the child instead.

A seventeen-year-old came for counseling. She was celebrating her 17th birthday but stopped to see her Granddad first and planned to celebrate with friends afterward. A man was waiting outside the senior center by her car and raped her. When she found out she was pregnant she didn't want to keep the children. She was pregnant with twins. It was the first adoption that took place at *Hope Center*. The twin boys looked like two beautiful cherubs and when the adoption was complete the parents left ecstatic.

A little girl from Ireland named Emma came to *Hope Center* with the police. A darling little four-year-old red head that was extremely shy, not making eye contact. Kathleen could see a scarf being tied around her neck by her father. A neighbor happened to come by, hearing screaming from next door. The police took the child and before they could get to the father, he shot himself. Apparently, his wife ran off with another man and he wanted to punish her by killing their daughter. The police confirmed what Kathleen saw.

Two brothers, ages nine and ten, lost their parents in a fire. Kathleen affectionately called them *double trouble*. She actually wanted to adopt them herself. Jax had to remind her that they couldn't adopt every child Kathleen wanted to bring home.

One day a little girl named Rachel from America came. Her mother died from cancer, and she had no other family. This case really hit Kathleen hard, and she did lots of healings to help her.

So many broken children. Some of the children responded quickly because they were relieved to be off the streets.

One boy aged seventeen named Davi lived with his younger brother Eli age ten. He lied about his age and got a job to take care of Eli. Nobody knew where their parents were. One day Davi took Eli to the beach. Davi was swept under a rip current and drowned. Eli had nobody and came to the group home. These stories could break your heart.

A young girl, Maureen, age 13, had to sleep with the light on, and even at that didn't sleep very well. Kathleen did a treatment on her and saw her locked in a dark closet by an abusive aunt that was her guardian. When Kathleen gently told the girl what she saw, and explained it was in the past, the girl could move on. She slept soundly from that day forward.

Momma and her auntie used their experience and wisdom to treat the children. They were a blessing to her along with her father, uncles, brothers, cousins, and Jax. She could have never done this undertaking by herself, and she was profoundly grateful. One thing all the children responded to, if only a little for the ones most battered, was knowing someone cared and would keep them safe from harm.

One mother that must have been breast feeding, left the baby in a basket at the front entrance of the building one morning. We assumed the baby was breastfed because there was a used breast pad under the child when she was picked up. The baby was obviously never bottle fed and the precious child screamed for her mother for three days uncontrollably. She was trying to find comfort from a nurse that was holding her by her breast.

One of the women in town, Brianna, had a nine-month-old baby she was trying to wean. He was a plump little boy with rosy cheeks.

 When she found out about the baby girl's situation, she volunteered to use a breast pump to nourish the child for as long as necessary. This brought tears to all the healers at *Hope Center*, and they all agreed there truly are angels among us.

Brianna showed up like clockwork every day to deliver the milk. One day she asked if she could feed the baby from the bottle. There seemed to be some kind of recognition between the two and the baby smiled up at her with sparkling blue eyes. This went on for another three months, and Brianna's husband also started to come with his wife to see the baby, after hearing so much about her.

One day Brianna and her husband Amon went straight to the office and said they wanted to adopt the little girl. They had three sons and Brianna longed for a little girl to dress in ruffles and put ribbons in her hair.

When the legalities were finalized, the whole family came. Their baby boy was too young to know what was going on, but the older boys kept giggling and taking turns gently kissing her on the top of her little head. They decided to name her Hope, after the center where they came to meet and fall in love with her.

Another child was admitted that was severely beaten. He had been tied to his bed with belts. He was only with us for a month and died a short time later. He had been starved and weighed only forty-five pounds at age thirteen. We all prayed that he would finally be at peace. The pain in his eyes haunted us. He was given healing treatments and IV nutrition but was too far gone. He lived with his aunt that had to be mentally deranged. She will spend the rest of her life behind bars unless one of the inmates kill her. As hardened as some of the prisoners are, they don't take kindly to hurting children.

Kathleen was in awe of most of these children. She realized now more than ever how lucky she was being adopted into such a loving family. Being orphaned at young ages carries unique struggles with the potential to teach others invaluable lessons.

If some of the children were willing to share their life stories at some point, Kathleen thought it would be extremely helpful to the others and give them hope to persevere.

Everyone that worked at *Hope Center* wanted the children to think of themselves as family, whether they stayed on or were adopted. Each child was given a notebook and asked to memorize the words on the cover. It was titled *Ohana* by Lilo and Stitch. *Ohana means family, and family means nobody gets left behind or forgotten.* They recited these words together out loud at the beginning of each class and before too long they were actually feeling it.

At Momma's suggestion they had a class on journaling. Sometimes getting your feelings out on paper is easier than speaking about it.

The following was the list of questions presented to the children to answer and repeated every few months to see if they gained more insight.

1. Who am I?

2. Does my life matter?

3. Is there a purpose to my life?

4. Where did I come from?

5. Am I important?

6. Will anyone ever love me?

The answers the children gave were great clues as to what was in their hearts, by the words they chose.

Finally, they were taught that what you feed your mind is just as important as what you feed your body.

The children enjoyed growing things in the garden. They loved watching their plants becoming ready to eat. Kathleen had a beautiful greenhouse nursery installed so they could grow things throughout the year. They were also taught about nutrition and what foods made you healthy and strong.

One day a week they had movie night with lots of buttered popcorn, and of course pizza.

They were also encouraged to get lots of exercise in whatever they enjoyed, such as dancing or sports. Everything at *Hope Center* was designed to nurture the children and prepare them for life.

Many of the children at *Hope Center* had been living on the streets and were happy to have a full belly. These children didn't take a warm bed for granted. Many were malnourished when they arrived. They seemed happy that people at the center actually smiled at them and made them feel welcome. Understandably, many had behavioral issues, anxiety, and depression.

Some kept waiting for their mothers to pick them up and didn't want to be adopted. They sadly didn't realize their mothers didn't want them and would never come back.

There were school buses that took the children to school and back. Kathleen made sure they all had nice clothing, shoes, backpacks and all the rest so they would feel like they fit in. They had choices of a packed lunch or were given money to buy it at the cafeteria.

For the children not emotionally ready to go to school, retired teachers self-lessly came five days a week to home school.

The children were grouped together with similar aged boys and girls, and many seemed to be becoming friends.

Kathleen set up a day camp which the children loved. Basically, it was parents that volunteered to be Boy Scout and Girl Scout leaders to teach them great life lessons. It was making a noticeable difference and they were taking pride in earning different badges.

Garrett and Finnegan were incredible at healing the children on the ranch with the horses. Sometimes, Kathleen thought horses must have invisible halos on their heads. She already knew for certain that Garrett and Finnegan did! The effect the healers had on the children's emotional as well as physical health-giving treatments was astounding.

She had gotten used to hearing "good mairning, lass" or "grand day isn't it, miss?" but the healers at the center had their own special language.

Kathleen especially loved how they greeted a person by saying *Namaste*, which also had such a beautiful meaning. *Namaste* was a Sanskrit word used as a greeting of respect and reverence. They placed their hands together by their heart with a slight bow toward another person.

Kathleen wanted to decorate all the rooms with uplifting wall art. She found one for the healing room with a plaque decorated in delicate pastel flowers that read:

Namaste
My soul honors your soul.
I honor the place in you
where the entire universe resides.
I honor the light, love, truth, beauty,
and peace within you because it is also within me.
In sharing these things, we are one.

The healers were the most love-filled people. They were so giving and shared their gifts without any reservation.

The children could feel it and responded, as there was no better medicine on earth than to be loved.

They were always picking little daisies from the garden and putting them in the children's hair.

Kathleen would find them among the nursery workers during their breaks, rocking and singing to the babies.

They surprised Kathleen one day with a surprise picture in the music room, showing musical notes in primary colors that read: Music is the divine way to tell beautiful, poetic things to the heart.

Babies were adopted in record numbers, and it was rewarding to all that worked at *Hope Center,* connecting all these beautiful families together.

Watching the adoptive parents leave with their child was the most incredible feeling in the world!

And the selfless women that opted out of having abortions and giving their babies to people that could better care for them were to be praised in the gift they gave to another human being.

Chapter Thirty-one

Two Years Later

$\mathcal{I}$t was hard to believe that *Hope Center* was in business for two years. Kathleen and Jax desperately wanted to have a baby but no luck yet.

Kathleen was going to be honored tonight at a banquet for her work as a philanthropist and humanitarian. All the folks came from the nearby farms and town. They still called her *Leigha* which meant *healer*. They were eternally grateful for the beautiful lass that healed so many, yet always remained humble, giving all credit to God.

She spotted Garrett walking in, holding a very pretty lady's hand. However, when she got up to speak, she saw a tear come down his eye. Kathleen didn't go to the farm much anymore and thought it was for the best. How many women were lucky enough in life to have two outstanding men love you? But Kathleen gave her heart away a long time ago in the Blue Ridge Mountains, gazing at the stars with Jax, when they were so young.

Finnegan was sitting in the front row with her family. And in case you might be wondering, yes, Fiona was sitting right next to him.

"Did I call that or what?" said Kathleen.

Kathleen walked on the stage, and everyone stood up out of respect and clapped. Kathleen, true to form, thanked all the people that made *Hope Center* such a success. She still didn't take credit, but instead thanked God and quoted her Momma Diane that "God always has a plan."

That evening when everyone went home, she had such a strong urge to walk up the hill where the sheep were grazing. One lamb walked straight over to her by the gate as she walked in. She started praying to God to allow her and Jax to have a baby together. Nothing was working and they both longed for a child of their own to love.

Suddenly the lamb disappeared and, in its place, stood Jesus. Kathleen was overcome with emotion. She remembered the scripture in John 10:2-4 *But to him the doorkeeper opens, and the sheep hear his voice, and he calls his own sheep by name, and leads them out. When he puts forth all his own, he goes before them, and the sheep follow him because they know his voice.*

Jesus spoke to Kathleen, "Very good Kathleen, you remember the Scriptures. Your pureness of spirit is what allows you to see me and hear my voice. Your prayer has been answered. Very soon, my daughter."

Jesus then vanished and Kathleen turned to walk back toward Jax, standing there waiting for her. He said she was glowing, and she shared her beautiful experience with her husband as they both just looked at one another with wonder, fully believing they would be having a baby to love.

Kathleen was happy to say that Garrett married the pretty girl he came to the banquet with a few months later. Garrett understood that her heart belonged to Jax. He also knew the special place they had in each other's hearts from all the experiences they shared her first year in Ireland.

It was time for him to move on. There was still a little awkwardness

Between them, but they both made it work as they would always be in contact with one another, and neither of them would ever cross the line by being unfaithful.

Chapter Thirty-two

Jax and Kathleen

*W*ell, they say life is full of surprises and boy is it!

Here's what happened:

Gabrielle said she would be traveling and away for a month. When we asked where she was going, she was very vague. She didn't want a ride to the airport either. We realized that she was entitled to her privacy, so we didn't question her any further. We told her to keep in touch, which she did, but very seldom. We were so busy with our lives that the days just seemed to fly by.

We stopped over one evening to visit Uncle Shawn and Garrett saw us. He came over to say that Shawn went on a trip but didn't mention where. Finnegan walked up behind Garrett and added that Shawn was acting almost giddy and told them he would be back in a month. They heard him whistling, walking toward his car.

Alarm bells started going off in our heads. Could they have possibly gone on vacation together?

Jax did notice that his mother seemed to be humming a lot, more lighthearted than usual and smiling nonstop.

Kathleen noticed that Gabrielle was cooking all of Shawn's favorite French and Vietnamese dishes for him. She even noticed his belly sticking out a little and thought he looked endearing. He was too skinny anyway.

Well so be it. If they were together, more power to them. Nothing would make us happier.

More surprises

When the month was nearly up, they called to tell us that they had a surprise and booked a flight back home the following Monday. We thought they were going to confess to us that they went on a vacation together. Well, that's kind of true. They did, but they also got married!

They spent the whole month in France. Uncle Shawn has actually been learning French and losing a little of his Irish lilt. Gabrielle on the other hand is developing a slight Irish accent as she has learned to repeat many Irish sayings that Shawn says.

Love is a many splendored thing.
-Andy Williams

Shawn wanted to propose to Gabrielle in the most romantic city in the world, which is Paris. He booked the Rooftop Terrasse Hotel for a month. They had a carefree relaxing time, laughed easily together, and even held hands going for long walks. Neither one was expecting to fall in love again, especially at this stage of their lives.

They visited charming cafés, old markets, and went to the Louver Pyramid, a favorite of art lovers, which Gabrielle was. They went to the Eiffel Tower at sunrise overlooking the Seine. That made their hearts feel peaceful and light.

Gabrielle was, of course, very fluent in French which was quite helpful. This was actually her first time in France, as she lived her whole life in Vietnam before marrying Jesse and moving to America.

Their last day in Paris they went to the Medici Fountains in the Luxembourg Gardens. Shawn specifically chose that spot to propose to Gabrielle because he read that although very romantic, it was also secluded. He was like a nervous teenager hoping for a "yes." He bought Gabrielle a brilliant diamond ring to put on her finger if she said "yes" and agreed to be his wife.

When he got the courage to ask, she made it very easy for him and told him she would be honored to be his wife. They shared a kiss that was filled with love and hope for a blessed future together.

They genuinely loved and cared for one another. Gabrielle knew that she would always be number one with Shawn. They knew it wasn't like young love but theirs was more compassion filled, with a wisdom kind of love. Jesse was Gabrielle's first love and Shawn was married a brief time, but his wife died suddenly from some unknown virus. She was also pregnant with his child. Shawn never wanted to experience that level of pain again, so he stayed single all those years. Gabrielle gave him the courage to take a chance and try again.

When they arrived back in Ireland, Jax and Kathleen arranged an intimate surprise wedding by the sea with just the Denari-Gianni family. Diane bought her a simple, exquisite, mint green, sleeveless fitted dress, as she knew Gabrielle's taste and size. Shawn had plenty of suits, so they bought him a tie to match her dress.

Darla and Momma were in the kitchen for days cooking up a storm. It was as though Grandma Kate was pushing them. The day they were making pies, we walked in the kitchen, and it was like de-ja vu.

The year we met in Grandma Kate's cabin, Diane and Darla had flour all over their faces making pies that time also. Jax teased them about being very messy bakers. They told him that he could get himself in front of the sink and start washing dishes. Kathleen giggled and got a towel to dry. She knew to never mess with Momma and Aunt Darla while they were baking.

When the newlyweds came through the door, Diane and Darla whisked Gabrielle by the hand into one of the bedrooms before even hugging the bride and groom.

David and Luca did likewise with Shawn. Talk about coming home and not having a clue what was happening. Shawn and Gabrielle didn't expect this kind of welcome. They didn't even know they were all coming to Ireland.

Unbeknownst to them, the whole Denari-Gianni clan was waiting at the beach to honor the couple.

All four of them managed to get the bride and groom to the wedding. No shoes necessary. The men took Shawn out a back door so he wouldn't see Gabrielle. They told him that he would understand in a few minutes and to please play along. They explained that it was Diane and Darla's idea, and both rolled their eyes muttering, "women."

Daphne started playing the song, *Unforgettable* by Nat King Cole, on her violin. Jax handed his mom her bouquet and walked her on a trail of rose petals to meet Shawn. The scene surrounding them on the side of the meadow was blooming in radiant red poppies as far as the eye could see. The weather couldn't have been more beautiful. A perfect Irish day by the sea!

The couple smiled almost shyly at one another. How did we not notice this? Isn't love wonderful! And it couldn't have happened to two kinder people. Dylan performed the ceremony and when he pronounced them husband and wife yet again, they kissed each other so sweetly, that we all got misty eyed.

The bride and groom were beyond touched that the whole family came in their honor. Plenty of hugs and kisses from everyone, followed by lots of great food and drinks. Sláinte! A true celebration of love!

Jax teased the mothers that everything tasted great except the pies, and started chuckling. Gabrielle swatted him on the back with a dishtowel, but all three were laughing.

Chapter Thirty-three

We're Pregnant

And baby makes three.

$\mathcal{K}$athleen was extremely tired with dark circles under her eyes and seemed to need more sleep than usual.

Jax was getting worried about her and asked her to please go to the doctor and get some blood work done. She promised that she would, but she suspected what was wrong. After trying for two years, she wanted to make sure before saying anything. She started to throw up, but used the bathroom down the hall, so Jax wouldn't hear her.

Her suspicions were confirmed by the doctor, and she was excited beyond belief, and wanted to be creative telling her husband.

Jax was packing for a business trip, so she tucked a onesie with *You're going to be a daddy* written on it. She also put a positive pregnancy test in his briefcase. He never mentioned anything, and she was puzzled how he never saw either one.

When he came home, she handed him a beer with a label that said, *Sleepless Nights*, and still nothing. The next morning, she gave him a coffee cup with

Sweet Surprise written on the bottom, but he didn't finish his coffee. For dinner she served his meal on a plate that said *We're pregnant!* but he didn't finish his food. What! How could he not see anything?

So, after dinner Kathleen said, "Honey how about playing Scrabble?"

"Sure baby," he responded.

She spelled out the letters once again with the words *having your baby*. He yawned and said he was sleepy and going to bed. She could see his shoulders shaking from behind. He knew all along! He was teasing her.

"Kathleen, I noticed you had some food left in the stove."

"I did?"

"Yes, I think it was a bun in the oven."

"You!" she said emphatically as she hurled a couch pillow at him. He scooped her up in his arms and told her he had never been more excited in his life.

"How did you know, Jax?"

"Are you kidding, our mothers both had the same dream that you were expecting and asked if it was true. You can never fool those two women."

What a blessing to this young couple to have their dream of being parents finally come true!

$$* * * * *$$

Boy or Girl

Kathleen's pregnancy was going very smoothly for the most part. They had an appointment with Dr. Murphy, her obstetrician, to find out the sex of their child. Jax and Kathleen both loved Dr. Murphy. He was known to sing to the newborn babies he delivered and was all heart.

Dr. Murphy had strict orders to call Gabrielle and Diane when he found out the gender, but not to tell Jax and Kathleen.

"How about just one little hint, Doc?" asked Jax.

They had no idea looking at the sonogram. They loved hearing the healthy heartbeat though.

Dr. Murphy was smiling and then answered Jax's question. "Do you want your mothers to cause harm to me?" and smiled again. We believe God hand-picked Dr. Murphy for his profession.

Jax and Kathleen were excited to get to the party and see their family. They couldn't wait any longer to find out what they were having. Kathleen wore an elegant pink dress and was glowing with good health and vitality. Jax wore a blue shirt and was ready to burst. He had been eating for two lately and was a wreck.

The Denari-Gianni family flew in from everywhere and the outdoor party was getting started in a nearby park. When Jax and Kathleen pulled up to the shelter they saw a huge banner in pastel colors that said, *Come For The Sex*. They both said out loud at the same time, "Aunt Darla!" and laughed.

Everything looked amazing! They had pink and blue badges that said *team girl* or *team boy* on the picnic table. There were balloons in different sizes arranged in a cluster in blue and pink with a few small gold ones sprinkled in.

They had the sweetest cake with white frosting and pastel trim with matching pastel baby blocks and balloons on top. There were all sorts of beautifully arranged, decorated hors d'oeuvres. Pastel cookies were in the shapes of carriages, rattles, and bibs with a little heart on each one. Everything looked outstanding!

Next to it were four large transparent blocks trimmed in white with pastel balloons in each one that spelled out B-A-B-Y on the far end of the table with drinks.

As usual, Finnegan and Fiona never disappointed. They had matching navy blue T-shirts with two ducks, one white, one pink in a white heart that said, *Waddle it Be?* Those two!

"It's time," someone shouted. Jax and Kathleen went outside, followed by everyone in great anticipation. They had two confetti cannons but had to wait to see what flew out. Only one color was inside, soon to be revealed, and only Diane and Gabrielle knew the gender.

Everyone shouted 1-2-3. Jax looked at Kathleen and said, "Ready Baby?"

"Ready!" she smiled back at her husband. They pulled on the cannons and beautiful pink hearts were flying in the air!

Jax kissed Kathleen and they were both beaming. They actually wanted a girl first but neither told the other because healthy was always the first choice.

Amazingly, most of the family had team girl badges.

Everyone came to hug the *mom and dad.*

And once again their beautiful, loud, wonderful family rejoiced for the next generation to arrive.

A little girl to lead the next family in the world someday.

*****

Cottage By the Sea

Jax and Kathleen were so excited that their new home would be ready in time for the baby. It was a cozy cottage by the sea but not very large and posh like you might expect. Jax and Kathleen were content with a smaller house.

The view was another story. The view of the sea was incredible. The house was white with byzantine blue shutters and a front door to match.

The best part was that it was very close to Uncle Shawn's. Of course, Kathleen planted some bluebells, daisies, and hollyhocks by the front entrance.

The interior was mostly creams and blues with warm wood furniture and flooring throughout. The ceiling had wide white wooden planks.

The family room had a blue linen gingham couch with solid blue matching chairs. The fireplace would be a nice touch in the Ireland winters.

The master bedroom was next to the nursery. It also had a fireplace and soft blue comforter with plush pillows. The window was large and had a window seat underneath in small blue checks that was perfect for curling up with a book. This house was all about comfort with the hopes of filling it with love, family, and friends for many years to come.

The baby's room had a white crib and changing table with cream walls. The drapery was pale pink to match a comfy pink chair for nursing the baby, and later to read story books.

Opposite the chair was a footstool made with tiny white jasmine flowers against pink linen material. The baby's comforter matched the footstool. Next to the crib, was a pale pink shelf with heart cutouts and little stuffed animals. They were so excited to meet their baby girl!

On the wall above the crib was a white framed picture that read, *Angels Danced the Day you Were Born.*

Lastly, an enormous fluffy rabbit that daddy came home with one day, sat in the corner of the room waiting for the baby's arrival.

Sometimes, Kathleen would sit on the chair with her hand over her stomach, dreaming about when the baby would actually be here in her arms. Jax would wander into the room knowing where to find her, and sit on the floor with his head on her lap.

Kathleen loved sitting on her cozy porch with the oak wood floor. She spent many days during her pregnancy sitting on the handsome acacia wood rocker that was perfectly curved, a gift from her Uncle Shawn. She was getting big as a house, but Jax loved it! She spent hours watching the clouds go by, reading her favorite books, and dreaming about the baby she and her husband were expecting. She was also enjoying a lot of ice cream which made Jax tease her good naturedly.

So much to be thankful for!

Chapter Thirty-four

Labor and Birth

*There is no force equal to that of a
determined woman giving birth.*

Kathleen

My contractions started at three a.m. and were pretty regular, so I woke up Jax and told him it was time to go to the birthing center. He had been sleeping with his clothes on the last few nights because I was having several intense Braxton Hicks contractions.

"I'm ready," he said and proceeded to get up as if he was a robot, grabbed my overnight bag and headed toward the car. I was stunned when I heard the car running. He actually got halfway to the birthing center and realized I wasn't in the car. How can you not laugh, I thought?

He came running into the house like it was on fire, apologizing profusely, and we started out again. Together this time!

Jax always made me laugh, even during labor, but he really tried his best to do the things taught by our mothers.

He gave me backrubs, told me how much he loved me, and how proud he was of me. We slow danced, swaying back and forth, when the midwife walked in.

"Ok you two, you can kiss all you want because it speeds up labor." We thought she was kidding but she was serious, so we gave it a try. I also squatted while Jax held my hand. Just then we heard the lady in the room across from us, screaming at the top of her lungs. The nurse walked in and informed her that she was making the other women scared. We saw the woman throw her cup of ice chips at the nurse and her aim was impressive!

The fun was over, and the pain was getting pretty intense, so I tried the best I could with *Coach Jax* to slow down my breathing.

He said, "Oh baby. My canker sore is killing me." I knew he didn't have a canker sore, he just wanted me to laugh.

When I was overheated, Jax put an ice pack on my forehead. When I was cold, he covered me with my soft, cozy blanket from home and rubbed my shoulders. He even got me into a bath with warm water that soothed me.

We also brought some relaxing aromatherapy oils to inhale. We were told to keep the lights dim, as more pain-relieving hormones are released in the dark.

By now, six hours had passed and Jax announced that his back and legs were cramping up from standing too long. Good thing he winked, or he would have been in a world of trouble.

It's amazing how the body knows what to do, and so much better when the fear is gone. The pain was raw and primal, but it was empowering to be a woman. I was in transition and the midwife was preparing the room with a bassinet and a tray of instruments for the baby's arrival.

When Jax saw that, his face turned white and the nurse said, "someone catch Daddy." They had to have Jax sit down while someone gave him some orange juice. He was embarrassed and told the nurse he had low blood sugar. I saw her smile. She told him that it happens a lot.

It was time to push, and the baby came out pretty smoothly, giving me a sense of euphoria. Jax was better now and actually cut the cord, with the midwife guiding him. Dr. Murphy held her for a few minutes, singing to her in a loving voice.

Our daughter was absolutely beautiful, and he laid her against me, skin to skin. Jax kept kissing me and the baby with so much love and absolute wonder. Our family of three.

*****

Jax

Having a baby with the woman you love was the most amazing, scary, wonderful experience of my life. I kept calling *the moms* on her progress. Uncle Shawn and Finn were pacing the halls like they were the fathers. God love those two men and how much they love Kathleen.

My wife is super fit and healthy, but I have never seen her so fierce and determined. I can't say the same for myself, almost passing out.

I really tried my best, but it was hard to see what my wife went through in labor. By the way, I really do have low blood sugar.

Seeing that precious little girl come out into the world and take her first breath gave me such a rush of love and protection. I vow to take the best care of my girls and always make it known to them how much they are loved.

Chapter Thirty-five

The Christening

Little baby fair and sweet,
On your Christening day.
A miracle of life so new,
Bonnie Lassie we love you.

Since all the family was in town, we decided to have a christening for our little Jasmine. Our two mothers bought Jasmine the most beautiful christening dress and little bonnet. She definitely looked like the star of the show today.

Of course, being a minister, Cousin Dylan would perform the ceremony. We had to do it at sunrise as all the family had flights back home to catch.

Jax and I decided to choose Finn and Fiona to be the baby's godparents. We loved all our brothers and cousins and thought it would be unfair to pick one over another.

So, we gathered in our backyard. The summer sky was filled with shades of sun filtering, peaceful, golden pink hues, where God's hand of artistry makes every day anew.

We could smell the scent of Irish roses from the yard and the sound of the ocean's rhythm swaying in and out in perfect harmony.

The family set up white chairs for everyone to sit. Each chair was capped in pale pink chiffon, tucked in back with a small bunch of jasmine flowers tied with white silk ribbons. We stood in front with Dylan while Finnegan and Fiona proudly held the baby. We had never seen these two so serious and had no doubt they would be incredible godparents.

Cousin Dylan performed a beautiful ceremony and had the godparents recite vows as their duties to look after the child.

Finn and Fiona were looking lovingly at the sweet baby that cooed in Fiona's arms. Dylan ended the service by telling the godparents that his prayer was for the two of them to be able to rejoice with all of Jasmine's accomplishments in life and encourage her walk with God. He added that she would always have a special place as the first person to begin their next generation.

Then Finn was, well Finn, and said to Dylan "You mean Jazzie," and everyone smiled.

Chapter Thirty-six

Airport Goodbyes

They all stopped to get lunch at the airport restaurant before going their separate ways. All agreed they were captivated by the beauty of the Emerald Isle!

Diane sighed with a dreamy smile on her face and said, "I am so in love with the baby. I just love to kiss those tiny hands."

"And how about those aqua blue eyes like my son's?" Gabrielle joined in.

David and Darla were quick to agree. David said, "Looks like another generation of blue eyes after my mother Kate and Jesse."

Being grandparents was a gift and all three went on and on describing the love they felt for Jasmine.

After about a half hour more of this, Darla and David had big smiles on their faces.

"What are you two grinning about?" Luca asked.

They all started to laugh, realizing all they ever talk about is the baby.

"Just you two wait," said Gabrielle. "It can't be helped," and they joined in with more laughter.

David said, "You all realize we are the *old folks* now and the oldest generation." David put his arm around Diane, feeling very sentimental. He said, "Diane I remember the first time you walked through the door with my brother Jesse."

"I remember," said Diane, "and you and your buddy Joey were playing toy soldiers with Hogan's Heroes blasting on the TV."

They both smiled remembering those carefree happy times. They went on discussing how their children were finding their own paths in the world and understood how their parents felt at the ages they were now. They all grew quiet and realized they were all thinking of Jesse sitting at the table with them. They never stopped missing him and all had an empty space in their hearts.

But life goes on. Some of the children were getting engaged and soon they would take their turn as the next generation, like it's been since time began.

They were starting to call the different destinations to depart, and all promised to get together soon. They hugged and wished each other safe flights home.

Gabrielle and Diane said they were planning another trip together to see Jax, Kathleen and the baby the following month.

Luca said, "Oh boy we are going to have one spoiled little girl on our hands." Truth was, he would be the worst of the bunch. Shawn would be flying to Seattle the following weekend. At the end of the month Gabrielle was going to be living full-time in Ireland with her new husband.

Chapter Thirty-seven

Special Delivery

Gonna take a sentimental journey
Gonna set my heart at ease
Gonna make a sentimental journey
To renew old memories
-Les Brown, Ben Homer, & Bud Green

After many months of trying to do the right thing, Uncle David, Aunt Darla, Kathleen, and myself decided to mail the diamond ring and letters I found in my father's bedroom that belonged to Diane. I put a little note inside the package saying that it was a group decision from all of us except my mother and I hoped we made the right one.

Diane

I was ready to get in the shower when I heard the doorbell ring. I was going to ignore it, but something told me it was important. The postman said he had a registered package for Diane Gianni. I answered that I was Diane and he handed me a pen to sign my name.

It was sent by overnight mail from Jax and insured for a hefty amount. I couldn't imagine what he could be sending me as I wasn't expecting anything.

When the postman handed me the package, I had goose bumps over my entire body. I had a flash back of sitting on Jesse's lap at the park, kissing him. It was the day before he left for AIT, and from there was sent straight to Vietnam.

We never had another chance to say goodbye and didn't see each other for a whole year. All of a sudden, I had more memories flooding my mind in fast motion, as though I was viewing the scenes on a movie camera.

I opened the package, and my hands were trembling. I saw a small velvet box that held a diamond. I noticed that it was engraved inside with the word *Je t'aime*, which was French for *I love you.*

I knew in my heart this was the ring Jesse bought to propose to me many years ago. I put it on my finger, and it fit perfectly. He probably asked my mother or sister Molly what size I wore, although strangely neither of them ever mentioned it to me.

The package contained old letters that I had written to him when he was in Vietnam. He saved every single one of them. I was very grateful that Luca was at the hospital because I needed to read them and process how I felt-- alone.

I read every one carefully and started to cry like I have never cried before in my entire life. The tears spilling out from my heart were unbearable. I had never realized the depth of grief that I carried for so many years. When Jesse died, I couldn't grieve as his widow because his wife was Gabrielle.

After reading the letters, I just sat there quietly for the longest time thinking about those beautiful carefree days when we were so young and in love.

I also remembered our last time together at Cyrena and Bradley's wedding and walking in the beautiful white flower garden together. Such a bitter-sweet evening and one my heart will never forget.

I put the letters in a drawer in my office because I wasn't ready to share them. It was the golden hour at the beach, so I found my sandals and went for a walk. The gulf breeze was soothing to my raw tender heart.

"Oh Jesse, we were just never meant to be," I whispered to myself.

More memories came, but this time they were the ones that caused me so much heartbreak. We were at an apple orchard drinking cider when he told me about Gabrielle being pregnant. I am not sure where I found the strength to walk back to the car.

I saw a dolphin up ahead and people pointing excitedly at the sight. The beach was such a happy place. The sun was ready to set soon, and I just stood in awe of the view of God's light show, and never tired of it.

I felt many times through the years since Jesse died, that he was with me, but never more than at this moment. I could almost feel his spirit next to mine. The diamond sparkled on my finger, and I thought it was such a pretty ring he chose and wondered if his mother Kate helped him pick it out.

I started walking back home and saw families admiring the sunset and heard the laughter of little children. I watched everyone enjoying life but wondered why Jesse was cheated with so many years left to live. "Why God?" I asked. "He was such a decent, loving man."

Sometimes, God's plan doesn't make sense to me. Some days were painful when my son Dylan became a teenager. What are the chances of a son looking identical to your first love and marrying his adopted brother? That had to be the biggest surprise of my life.

I stopped to rest and found an empty bamboo hut with a bench. I decided to sit under it and watch the sunset. I started to wonder what life would have been like if Jesse and I were married and sharing a family together. I never in all the years past would allow myself this thought. More tears came and I sobbed hard for everything we lost.

I am forever grateful that Jax sent me the ring and letters as they are precious gifts to my very soul.

I will call him later to thank him and tell him the package arrived safely.

It was getting dark, and the sky turned indigo blue. The cottage lights were all turned on now, leaving a golden glow.

I saw Luca waving and walking toward me. He must have just gotten home from the hospital, so I slipped the ring in my pocket.

I waved back at my darling, *Old Man Gianni*, as I still called him. I realized at that very moment how truly blessed I was to love and be loved by Luca and Jesse in my lifetime. I ran to my husband, hugged him tightly, and we walked home hand in hand.

At some point I will share this part of my life with Luca but will always consider the diamond ring and letters an incredible gift to my heart from my Jesse. I wondered if he orchestrated it from above.

Someday I will pass down the ring to my granddaughter and tell her about a real fairy tale story that happened when a young boy and girl fell deeply in love one night after a football game in a diner, and it was love at first sight.

Chapter Thirty-eight

Life with Baby

*J*ax and Kathleen were sitting on their front porch finishing a cup of tea after dinner and relaxing, as a gentle rain fell with the sweet smell of the earth and honeysuckle that grew close by.

Kathleen was nursing their newborn baby and she and Jax talked about how blessed they were to have each other to love, and their beautiful daughter. Jax adored his wife and treasured their life together.

Kathleen noticed Jax was getting sleepy and said, "Go to sleep love. Your flight for work leaves early tomorrow." The last of their family left that morning after Jasmine's christening.

This would be Jax's last flight as he found a very lucrative position close by. He wanted to spend every moment with his little family. They both never stopped being grateful that Jax's life was spared in that horrible airplane crash.

He kissed his wife on her forehead and then kissed his daughter. The baby was looking up at Kathleen with those beautiful aquamarine eyes like Jax's and holding her little hand curled around her thumb.

Kathleen was feeling very sentimental tonight about family. She smiled thinking of her ornery brothers and loved that they visited so often and even came shortly after she gave birth. She looked into her daughter's eyes and said, "I have so many stories to share with you about growing up with four brothers. Lord, the trouble those four got into!

"Also, my five cousins and Uncle David and Aunt Darla. It was a relief that three of them were girls!

"You were born into a family that knows hardships but also great love. One day I want to tell you about your da's father, Jesse, and what an incredible man he was.

"I will share stories about your great grandparents, Steve and Kate, that were the salt of the earth which were your da's clan, and Momma Diane's parents, Pastor Mike and Emily, that were the most wonderful souls.

"I will tell you the story about your Aunt Molly and how she met her husband Marcus at Momma Diane and my father Luca's wedding. Their last name is Malone. Isn't Molly Malone a posh name?

"You will always know your Irish heritage about my da, Liam, and mam, Shannon, along with Uncle Shawn and Gran Grace.

"Your great, great Gran Bette was an amazing healer and left me her Claddagh ring that will go to you next. And I have so many of my own adventures to share too, my precious one.

"Momma Diane, my father Luca, and my Tante Gabrielle, which I now call Maman, to honor her French heritage, all came in plenty of time after your birth and fussed all over you. I have no idea where I am going to fit all the gifts they keep buying you! I was blessed to have a pediatrician for a father and two mothers in the medical field that knew everything to make your natural birth easier.

"My *Bonnie Lassie*, wherever you go in God's world, stay connected to family by love. Remember that love is a journey and when it's too heavy to carry alone we will carry it together.

"It will be surprising what you remember years later, a certain conversation, perhaps a place you visited, your first kiss. For me that was your da.

"Know how lucky you are when you find love and never settle for ordinary love. Look for someone that can speak right to your heart without saying a word, while touching your soul. And don't forget laughter, so you can share joy and carefree days with one another. This will make the hard times easier.

"Life is simple but never easy. Be the next generation to weave another layer to the tapestry, where you add your own thread woven in to share with the kin that come after you. Remember your roots."

The baby seemed to be getting sleepy, but in some strange way seemed to understand Kathleen's words. Kathleen continued after gently kissing the top of her sweet head and breathing in her scent.

"I love a quote by Anita Opper...*Everywhere in everything is everyone who has ever been. We are surrounded by their energy, their spirits, their love.*

"I pray I will live to dance at your wedding one day, as my mam and da died young. But if not, I will be celebrating in heaven and pray God's joy rests on your heart. Jasmine, remember that you will be the first person to lead the next generation. Wear your name proudly.

"I love the name your da actually chose for you. Jasmine. It suits you, as you are pretty as a little flower. My bonus brother, Finn, calls you Jazzie. I chose the name Grace as your middle name after my Gran Grace, so you were christened Jasmine Grace Denari.

"May you feel God watching the birth of a baby lamb, or the beauty of wildflowers blooming in the spring. Never lose the wonder of a soft golden sunrise or the pinks, purples, and golds of a sunset. These are all gifts from our Creator.

"There is a saying to *bloom where you are planted*. I don't believe that is true. You can take four flowers and plant them in four different directions. One might die, one grow slowly, one always drooping from too much sun, and the fourth blossom to great heights of exquisite beauty with little care.

"Remember in your life, my little one, what Momma Diane taught me to be true. *God always as a plan.* Live where you blossom, no matter where that takes you in this great big world. Trust God, and like a flower, you will have a season to bloom!"

Novels give us the ability to have a front row seat inside a person's soul, possibly changing the way we view our own lives. That's why we may think of the characters long after we read the last page, and forever be changed within.

About the Author

Deborah had been a healer for nearly thirty years when God led her to Isaiah 55:11, with the understanding that it was His plan for her to write books. It began with a book she coauthored, titled *Seeds of the Shepherd*. She became an award-winning author, writing in different genres.

Poetic Parables, Celebrating God in Nature, was written during many months of being in the Presence of the Divine, as though taking a walk in God's garden. It won silver in the poetry division from Illumination Book Awards for exemplary literature in Christian books.

She also won the Purple Dragon Fly award in children's literature for her chapter book in poetry, titled *Puppies, Kids, and Caterpillars*. It sends a sweet, whimsical message to children of being loved in a nature setting.

Her second children's book, a laugh-out-loud comedy, co-authored with her grandchildren, is titled *Farting Baba and Grandkids*. It won the prestigious Mom's Choice Award, globally recognized for excellence in family-friendly media.

Her first novel, *First Kiss, Last Kiss*, is a story about young love at first sight, in the backdrop of Viet Nam, spanning three generations. Even though fate changed their lives, the invisible bonds of love can never be broken.

Bloom, The Next Generation, is the sequel to *First Kiss, Last Kiss*.

Deborah's books are all written from the heart for all her readers.

Dear readers,

I hope you enjoyed reading book two of the series, *Bloom—The Next Generation,* as much as I did writing it.

Please give a like or review on Amazon or Barnes & Noble.

I also welcome you to visit my author page under Deborah D'Antonio on Facebook or follow me on Amazon's Author Central.

Thank you!